SHE LONGED FOR, ACHED FOR, HIS EMBRACE....

"Oh, Cass," she breathed softly, "let's not waste any more time."

His lips crushed hers, then moved over them in an erotic blending of motion and rising passion that joined them in an ecstasy of shared feeling. Pulling her against his hard warmth, Cass's hands found their way beneath her sweater, traveling over her in sweet torment. This was what she had waited for, hoped for, all evening. She wanted him to touch her, caress her, to blot out reality, until nothing else mattered. She had never wanted anyone like this before, even in her wildest dreams....

KASEY ADAMS is an incurable romantic who loves to travel, paint, and, above all, write. She also enjoys numerous activities, including working as an Emergency Medical Technician, and teaching kindergarten. Ms. Adams is the mother of two grown children and lives in California with her husband. She is the author of another Rapture Romance, Untamed Desire.

Dear Reader:

It's a new Rapture! Starting this month we'll be bringing you only the best four books each month, by well-known favorite authors and exciting new writers, and to demonstrate our commitment to quality we've created a new look for Rapture: bigger, bolder, brighter. But don't judge our books by their covers—open them up and read them. We've used the comments and opinions we've heard from *you*, the reader, to make our selections, and we know you'll be delighted.

Keep writing to us. Your letters have already helped us bring you better books—the kind you want—and we depend on them. Of course, we are always happy to forward mail to our authors—writers need to hear from their fans!

And don't miss any of the inside story on Rapture. To tell you about upcoming books, introduce you to the authors, and give you a behind-the-scenes look at romance publishing, we've started a *free* newsletter, *The Rapture Reader*. Just write to the address below, and we will be happy to send you each issue.

Happy reading!

> The Editors
> Rapture Romance
> New American Library
> 1633 Broadway
> New York, NY 10019

WINTER'S PROMISE

by
Kasey Adams

RAPTURE ROMANCE
NEW AMERICAN LIBRARY

PUBLISHER'S NOTE

This novel is a work of fiction. Names, characters, places, and incidents
either are the product of the author's imagination or are used fictitiously,
and any resemblance to actual persons, living or dead, events,
or locales is entirely coincidental.

NAL BOOKS ARE AVAILABLE AT QUANTITY DISCOUNTS
WHEN USED TO PROMOTE PRODUCTS OR SERVICES.
FOR INFORMATION PLEASE WRITE TO PREMIUM MARKETING DIVISION,
THE NEW AMERICAN LIBRARY, & COMPANY, 1633 BROADWAY,
NEW YORK, NEW YORK 10019.

Copyright © 1984 by Valerie Whisenand

All rights reserved

SIGNET, SIGNET CLASSIC, MENTOR, PLUME, MERIDIAN AND NAL BOOKS
are published by The New American Library, & Company,
1633 Broadway, New York, New York 10019

First Printing, March, 1984

1 2 3 4 5 6 7 8 9

PRINTED IN THE UNITED STATES OF AMERICA

*To my Joe,
and to Edith Reeder,
a very special lady*

Chapter One

The young, bearded man climbed lightly up the steep, curving slope, despite his cumbersome backpack. Running his fingers through his sandy brown hair, Dr. John Cassidy shaded his deep blue eyes and smiled at the sight of the quaint mountain town. Julian, California, had been a favorite stop on his rambling hikes ever since he had joined the staff of the nearby observatory two summers ago.

Thank God, Elizabeth had had the foresight to choose a spring wedding, he thought ruefully. I'd have frozen to death in December, trying to escape the inevitable and having to attend the gala affair with my colleagues. Weddings on the observatory grounds were rare. How much easier it would have been for all concerned if she'd decided to have the ceremony in town.

Elizabeth. He shrugged. At least it would all be over by the time he finished his vacation and returned to the observatory and his work. Sadness started to invade his thoughts, and he fought the melancholy.

"No," he said aloud.

The enormous black dog at his side looked inquiringly up at him.

"Not you, Bear," he assured the animal tenderly, "I'm afraid I was talking to myself."

Cassidy's jaw clenched as the memories of his former love invaded his mind. Elizabeth had hurt him deeply. Someday, he knew, he would get over her enough to seek out another relationship, but not now. Not yet. Solitude, clean air, simple good food, beautiful country, and a faithful dog for company—that was all he needed or wanted. It was enough for any man.

Speaking of dogs, where had Bear disappeared to? A speck of black vanished around a corner at the top of the steep grade. No, he thought, it couldn't be. Bear never got that far ahead. He must have ventured out of sight behind some chaparral.

The sound of her own scream shocked Laurel Phillips as much as it did her adversary. He froze momentarily, then sought to clamp his burly hand over her mouth as the piercing sound continued.

Screaming was definitely not a professional response to the man's improper advances, Laurel thought. It was a ridiculous way to deal with Frank. It was a helpless woman's way out, it was . . .

Laurel ducked, frantically trying to avoid his grasp and escape through the open door of the storage shed, but his body effectively blocked her way.

WINTER'S PROMISE

She had found Frank loathsome right from their first meeting two days before, with his suggestive glances, veiled insinuations, and disgusting mannerisms, but this—this was unthinkable. Despite all her training as a psychologist, Laurel had been cornered by the most revolting man she could ever remember meeting, and her prospects of escape didn't look promising.

Now what? she thought. Her heart pounded, echoing in her ears, throbbing in her temples. Laurel gasped for air through her tight throat. Dear Lord! After all the individuals she had dealt with and helped, was this going to be the one person she couldn't handle? Thoughts of what Frank might have in mind for her were too horrible to dwell on. She had to get out of the shed.

A dark form flashed through the open doorway, brushing against her legs. Knocked off balance, Laurel struggled to stay on her feet. If she fell, she'd have no chance at all against Frank's strength and bulk. None. The room swam before her eyes like a surrealistic nightmare as she flailed her arms, reaching for anything that would support her. Grasping the edges of some cardboard boxes, she finally righted herself.

Frank had stopped moving. He stared, frozen in his tracks. "Call off the dog, or you'll be sorry," he warned, his yellowed teeth displayed in a snarl.

Dog? Of course, a dog, but so big! Laurel steadied herself on her feet while the huge dog placed himself in front of her, glaring menacingly at Frank.

Reaching for a crowbar hanging on the wall of the

shed, the swarthy man raised it over his head. "Call him off, or I'll bash his skull in."

That seemed to be enough to fully convince the enormous animal of his duty. Inch-long fangs appeared as the dog curled back his lips, emitting a deep, unmistakably sinister growl. Seeming to grow even larger with his hackles raised, the dog stepped forward slowly, every muscle in his one hundred and eighty pound body tensed for attack.

Frank's fist tightened around the crowbar, his knuckles blanching from the effort. Color drained from his face. "I mean it," he spat, his voice beginning to lose some of its earlier assuredness, "I'll kill him."

Eyeing the confrontation, Laurel seriously doubted Frank would win, should it come to that. Still, there was no need to find out. The dog had evened the odds in her favor, and she knew it.

Laurel bravely stepped forward, resting her trembling hand on the animal's smooth head. "No, you won't," she said calmly, "you're fired."

She knew, the moment she spoke the words, that terminating his employment was a last resort. Rob and Joan had entrusted the management of their little market to her, instructing her to rely on Frank to get her over the rough spots. Now, she had irrevocably ended the uneasy truce between herself and the dreadful man, but under the circumstances there was nothing else to do. In the light from the door, Laurel saw his mouth drop open.

"You'll never make it without me, Miss High and Mighty," he hissed. "You with your fancy clothes, college degrees, and snooty ways. This whole business will fall apart!"

Laurel's stomach was churning, but she kept an even tone. "I'd rather fail than spend one more minute with you. Now, get out."

Frank leaned toward Laurel. The dog was growling, his fangs bared. Even an arrogant idiot like Frank wasn't fool enough to pit himself against those teeth.

"All right. You win, for now," he hissed. The crowbar landed noisily among the crates as he started for the door, and the huge dog jockeyed to keep himself between Laurel and Frank's unleashed anger. "You'll be sorry," the man tossed back. Then he was gone.

Following him as far as the door, the big animal watched his departure, then returned to a quivering Laurel Phillips. His wide, pink tongue licked her clammy hand, and his full, bushy tail greeted her like an old friend.

Laurel sank to her knees on the dusty floor, draping one arm around the dog's furry neck and looking into the beneficent face. Deep, brown eyes shone calmly into her misty hazel ones while the dog panted affectionately.

"Well," she said, "wherever you came from, I'm glad you decided to help. I hate to admit it, but that was the tightest spot I've ever been in." She relaxed into a sitting position on the ground, mindless of her good gabardine slacks or beige suede pumps. The dog towered over her and she looked up at his majestic bulk. "You're bigger than I am," she marveled. "And you're gorgeous, not to mention courageous and intelligent. I'm glad you didn't like him, either," she said, patting her rescuer. The resulting wag of the dog's tail nearly bowled her over.

Laughing, Laurel climbed unsteadily to her feet. That, she told herself again, was a close call. Putting a hand to her chest, she tried to still the pounding of her heart. Her mouth was dry and an incipient headache lurked beneath her temples. She took one deep breath, then another. Vaguely, she thought she heard a man's voice calling someone. Her huge companion cocked his head, then tucked his magnificent tail between his hocks and fairly tiptoed to the door on feet the size of Laurel's fists.

"Hey, wait for me, boy," she stammered nervously, running a slim hand quickly over her soft auburn curls and smoothing her rumpled outfit. "You and I are together, remember?"

With a tiny wag of his tail, the dog glanced up at her, his head still lowered in subjection.

They stepped out into the warm, spring sunlight: a subdued, black behemoth and a small, slightly built, and very dusty lady.

"Bear! Damn your fuzzy hide." The breathless Dr. Cassidy half jogged, half stumbled up the slope to the shed. "I thought I'd lost you." Perspiration trickled slowly down his temples to be stopped in its descent by the curly hairs of his short, sandy-colored beard and mustache. A plaid flannel shirt strained over his powerful, broad shoulders, and his worn jeans clung to the hard muscles of his thighs. From the effect it had on his momentum, the large, blue backpack he carried was obviously overloaded.

"Oops!" he exclaimed as he barely avoided a collision with an already-frazzled Laurel. His eyes were inexorably drawn to his dog, standing like a gentle black giant, barely wagging his tail and pleading with his eyes for forgiveness and understanding. "Bear, what possessed you?" the weary man asked, lifting his gaze to Laurel. "I'm sorry, miss, he—Oh, my God!"

Her silky, shoulder-length hair was festooned with cobwebs, and her usually impeccable outfit was a mass of dust, the place where she had sat down in the shed clearly outlined on the seat of her pants.

Leaning over gingerly, Cassidy peered at her first from one side, then the other, trying his best to stifle a grin. He cleared his throat to regain his composure.

"I, ah, I really am sorry," he said. "Bear is usually such a calm dog. His actions are as much a surprise to me as they are to you. This is the first time in the five years I've had him that he's disobeyed. I hope you're not hurt." He finally let his smile erupt and Laurel watched it spread across his handsome face, illuminating his countenance with a glowingly honest warmth and penetrating his twinkling blue eyes.

Had she been blindfolded, Laurel felt she would still have noticed his rugged masculinity; he exuded it like an overpowering fragrance. For a moment, she stood in rapt silence, watching his charismatic smile. He wasn't overly tall, just about right, she thought, before censoring her observations. Good grief. Now why did I think that? Amazing. She supposed she would be an unusual woman if she didn't at least notice a well-built, good-looking man when she saw one. He was definitely both of these. A warm flush stole over Laurel, but Cassidy didn't appear to notice.

He went on. "Please, miss, don't hold it against the dog. He, um, he's just a might too playful sometimes."

Sensing he was the object of his master's conversation, the big dog was beginning to wag his tail again.

Cassidy bit his lower lip, trying to control his growing amusement. At least Laurel thought he did. It was awfully hard to tell with all that hair on his face. She raised her eyebrows rather haughtily, looking him over from head to toe.

With a flourishing bow, he met her gaze, a lop-sided grin twisting his lips impishly. "Don't look down on poor travelers, miss. We do the best we can with what nature provides."

"You go around living off the land?" Laurel was appalled at his apparent lack of social consciousness.

He nodded affirmatively. "Maybe that's what's wrong with Bear's company manners."

A vagabond. Laurel had heard of men who spent their lives on the road, but she'd never actually met one until now. Squaring her shoulders, she took the corner of her light brown butcher's apron, the mundane badge of her new office at the market, and swiped at her face. Unknown to her, she only disarranged one patch of dirt and added another.

"You are quite mistaken," she said, remaining aloof. "Your gallant animal came to my rescue." She would

WINTER'S PROMISE

see that this ne'er-do-well stopped laughing at her. The whole thing was decidedly *not* funny.

"Well, Bear," he said, patting the huge, squarish head, "good for you." Turning to Laurel, Cassidy looked her up and down more seriously as his dog sauntered off to lie in the shade. "Is there anything I can do for you, or did my dog finish the job?"

"Thank you, I'm fine now," she replied calmly.

"Good. My name is Cass—and yours?"

Laurel hesitated. "Why would you want to know that?"

He shrugged his shoulders, then loosened the pack and let it slide to the ground. "No reason. I just thought that when Bear got around to writing his memoirs, it would be nice to know the names of all the damsels he had rescued."

"I may have been rescued," she bristled, "But I'm no damsel. I'm a psychologist."

The absurdity of her statement, under the present circumstances, brought a resounding laugh from Cass. "A what?" he howled. "Oh, come on. You don't look old enough to be out of college yet. Besides, since when do psychologists go crawling around in sheds?"

He wouldn't take her seriously. Well, she'd see about that. "When they're being attacked," Laurel said crisply. "And I'm twenty-six, thank you."

Cass's smile faded. "You mean it, don't you? Hey, I am sorry. Is the guy gone?" He pivoted, glancing over to the street.

"I—I think so," she answered. "He left in a big hurry when your Bear showed up." Frank *was* gone, but Laurel felt her body start to react again to the scene in the shed. Anger was senseless, she knew, but she felt it wash over her in an intensity that was difficult to control. She clenched her fists against the helpless feelings her fury generated.

"Where's the man now?" Cass pressed.

"I don't know."

"Look, miss . . ."

"Phillips," she said, "*Ms*. Laurel Phillips."

"Look, *Ms*. Phillips," he said with a ghost of a smile, "if I were you, I'd get back inside and phone a friend, or the police, or someone."

She eyed Bear. "Want to rent your dog?" she asked him. "I don't know a soul in Julian—except for the help at the store, that is, and I only met them two days ago."

"You're kidding," he replied, astonished, "No one?"

"No one." Laurel's problem was starting to grow in her fertile mind. Wherever Frank had gone, it probably wasn't far, but even with a thousand miles between them she wouldn't feel safe. An idea tugged at the edges of Laurel's consciousness—not a permanent solution, but certainly a viable temporary one. It might not be the answer she would have liked, but "any port in a storm," as Grandma used to say. "Listen, Mr.—ah—Cass," she began. "Since your dog did get me out of a touchy situation, let me repay you both with lunch." Surely, their presence would help stave off further incidents for a time, at least until she could gather her wits and plan her next move.

"Thanks, but no thanks," Cass said politely. "And the name is Cassidy. Cass is a nickname."

"But, Mr. Cassidy," Laurel stammered, "you wouldn't turn down a free meal, would you? I mean, a man in your position must—" She broke off, flustered. Laurel didn't want to offend him, but she had to convince him to stay.

"My position, Ms. Phillips?" he said formally, "Just what do you imagine my position to be?"

"Well, you are on the road, and . . . and you do live out of that thing," she said, pointing to his pack, "don't you?"

"Yes, I do. So?"

"So why turn down lunch? I'm sure your poor dog would accept, if he could express his opinion."

Cass and Laurel both glanced over at Bear's rotund form, relaxed into a lazy pile of slowly breathing fur.

"Sure," Cass noted, "he's skin and bones, right?"

"Well, no, but . . ."

Sensing that he was, again, the object of their undivided attention, the dog raised his head, yawned cavernously, and thumped his tail.

Chuckling, Cass cocked his head toward the dog. "I believe he's chosen to stay, Ms. Phillips, and since Bear is the hero around here, I'll accept his decision. Would you like us to wait out here?"

"Oh, ah, well, yes. I guess I'd better tell Sandy, too, before I break for lunch. She's running the cash register up front." Laurel smoothed the brown apron tied around her slim waist. "I'm temporarily managing the store," she explained unnecessarily.

Cass smiled slightly. "I guessed something like that. Look, if you're busy, why don't we just forget it? I carry my own provisions, and I really should be leaving if I'm going to make my next planned stop."

Placing her hand gently on his arm, Laurel sought to reassure him. "No, really, it's no trouble, and I will feel so much better if you'll stay. Just consider it a reward for a job well done." His arm was rock-hard yet warm, and she felt a surprising tingle start at her fingertips, traveling like lightning up her arm to suffuse her whole body.

"You mean by Sleeping Beauty over there?" Cass said sarcastically, nodding at his dog.

Bear trotted slowly up to Laurel and nuzzled her free hand.

"Fine thing," Cass said dryly. "I plan our itinerary, do all the work, and he gets to kiss the beautiful girl. There's no justice." A small smile was beginning to curl his lips, lifting the corners of his mustache as he spoke.

Laurel withdrew her hand from Cass's arm. "Justice, Mr. Cassidy?" she snapped, "If there were any real justice in this world, people wouldn't go around hurting one another." I'm lucky, she mused seriously, that my problem with Frank was solved so easily. She shivered, remembering.

The smile faded from Cass's face as he watched her closely, quietly.

"Uh, listen," Laurel said, returning to the present. "You go ahead and wait out here. I'll call you when the food is all set up."

Cass watched her turn and hurry through the back door into the market, her lithe body still coated with dust in some rather disconcerting places. Raising his eyebrows, he ran one hand through his sandy hair and sat down heavily on the porch, next to Bear.

"Well, boy," he said pensively to the sleepy dog, "now you've done it." Leaning his elbows on the knees of his faded jeans and clasping his hands, Cass sighed, "That little lady is the last thing I need right now, and you've put us right in the middle of her problems. Thanks a bunch."

Bear's tail flopped happily against the stoop as he stretched out and closed his eyes, the image of pure contentment.

Chapter Two

A cold sweat washed over her, and Laurel had to support herself against a stack of soda cartons. Glancing at her reflection in the glass doors of the refrigerated dairy case, she noticed that her naturally wavy hair looked more unkempt than usual, but she hardly cared. Her body's physical reactions caught up with her, and the events of the last half hour were beginning to take their toll. Laurel shook, feeling weak, and panic sawed at her emotions.

"I'm all right. I'm all right," Laurel repeated as she took a few deep breaths. "I've got to pull myself together. It's all over.

A past master at covering her true feelings, she soon regained most of her self-control. She stared at her reflection once again, this time searching for any wayward signs of surface turmoil. Satisfied, she straightened her apron, pushed back the stray wisps of her hair, and walked purposefully down the aisle to the front of the store. She was fine now, just fine, she told herself. As usual, she was just fine.

"Listen, Sandy," Laurel began as she reached the cash register, "there's a fellow out back that I've promised a free lunch. Do you mind if I take my break now?"

The younger girl looked up from the case of cigarettes she was using to fill the rack. "No problem, Laurel." Sandy's eyes widened. "What happened to you?" she gasped.

Still a little unsteady in spite of her resolve, Laurel leaned against the counter. "Frank," was all she said.

Gritting her teeth, the clerk nodded. "Welcome to the club. Are you okay?"

"Well, considering everything that could have happened and didn't," Laurel replied, "I'm great." She looked at the counter. "Oops. I forgot the bags I went after."

"I never should have let you go out to the shed alone knowing the way Frank is. It's just that you seemed so . . . so, in charge of everything, I never thought—I'm really sorry," Sandy said penitently.

Laurel saw tears begin to cloud Sandy's vision. "Hey, it's all right, Sandy," she assured the girl. "I was rescued in the nick of time, just like in the movies."

"By the free lunch?" Sandy asked, beginning to show curiosity.

"Well, yes and no," Laurel explained. "By the free lunch's dog."

Sandy laughed. "His dog?"

"You wouldn't laugh if you'd seen the dog. He's magnificent."

"And Mr. Free Lunch?"

A wry smile twisted one corner of Laurel's mouth. "He's, well, he's different, that's for sure. I guess you'd say he's sort of a hobo, only young. He looks to be about thirty-two or thirty-three."

Sandy leaned over, peering down the nearest aisle. "Where is he? This I've got to see."

"There's not much to see," Laurel replied dryly, "unless you like tall, hairy men." And warm, and friendly, and attractive, and physically very appealing, she added silently. Laurel smiled, unconscious of how Sandy might interpret the look on her face.

Sandy began to giggle.

Laurel blushed, suddenly aware. "I didn't mean—I mean—oh, skip it."

Laughing, Sandy couldn't resist the chance to tease her new boss. "Uh oh, you're getting very embarrassed. What is it with you and this guy, anyway?"

"The dog is adorable, Sandy, but the man is a wanderer. He's definitely not my type," Laurel insisted. The man was, however, more male than anyone she'd encountered for some time. Put him in a decent business suit and he might prove to be the most intriguing man she had ever met. She shrugged. Too bad he had chosen to waste all that potential.

"Okay, okay, take your lunch break now," Sandy prodded, "but expect to see me sneaking a peek at this hairy beast of yours."

Laurel turned on her heel, hurrying up the aisle. "He's not *my* beast, young lady, and you can consider yourself chained to that cash register until further notice," she teased. "Now, back to work while I go get the dust washed off and put on a fresh apron."

Saluting with a flourish and a broad grin, the young cashier went reluctantly back to her chores.

I wonder what he likes to eat? Laurel thought. She chuckled. Wild nuts and berries was the first thing that popped into her mind. And tree bark, she added, beginning to laugh. I'll bet there's not a processed or synthetic snack in any of his provisions. Oh well, she decided, one meal from civilization won't pollute him too badly.

Gathering up an armload of food, Laurel spread it out on several cases of paper towels, pulled up two crates for chairs, and called out the door, "Come and get it—both of you."

Cass peered inside. "Both of us?" he repeated. "I don't think dogs are supposed to come into stores."

"You're right," she admitted ruefully. "Okay, here, take this out to Bear, then come and make yourself a sandwich."

Bear gratefully accepted the plate of dog food. Making sure his dog had drinking water, Cass shouldered his pack and entered the market. "Do you have somewhere I could wash up?" he asked. "I've been on the road for quite a while."

So I gathered, Laurel thought, but said only, "Sure. Through there," and pointed to the restrooms. She couldn't help noticing the snug fit of his faded jeans on his lean hips, and the way he moved. Without the pack, he seemed almost graceful, in an animalistic sort of way. Laurel was still staring at the door when he came back through it, the sleeves of his plaid shirt rolled up to expose bare, slightly freckled forearms.

The hair at the back of his neck curled softly over his collar. Except for the beard, she decided, he's really a rather nice looking man.

"Do I pass inspection?" he teased, seating himself across from her and smiling broadly.

"I beg your pardon?" Laurel asked, coming out of her reverie.

"Well, you seemed to be looking me over, so I thought I should ask if I was acceptable."

Crimson color rose to her cheeks.

"A woman who blushes," he remarked. "Now that's a welcome sight these days. Most girls hardly flinch anymore."

"I told you," Laurel insisted, "I'm not a girl, I'm a psychologist."

Cass picked up a piece of bread, spreading mustard lavishly across it. "Oh, you're a girl, all right. I haven't been on the road so long that I've forgotten how to tell."

"Baloney!" Laurel said, handing him a package of lunchmeat. He certainly was bold for having known her for such a short time.

"Is that an opinion, or are you telling me what to eat?" he teased.

"Both."

"Fair enough." Cass plastered another piece of bread with mayonnaise and took out slices of meat from the package, completing his sandwich. "Now," he said, "while I eat my reward, you can tell me what a lady psychologist is doing crawling around a storeroom with some local lecher."

Laurel sighed. "It's a long story."

"Undoubtedly. But please, talk slowly so there's enough time for me to have a second sandwich," he said, biting hungrily into the first.

"Okay," she began, "I live and work in Ohio."

"Boy, are you lost," Cass interjected. "That must be some commute."

Laurel made a face. "Anyway," she said, "I have this friend, Joan, from school. This is her store, and like a dummy I said if she ever needed someone to help out she should call on me."

"And she did?"

"You got it. We've kept in touch since we both got out of school. She married Rob and moved out here, while I went on to get my master's."

"Very impressive," Cass muttered, taking a final bite.

"Thanks. To make a long story shorter, Rob and Joan finally saved enough to go to Australia on a second honeymoon, and when they needed someone to look after their business, Joan thought of me. Thank heavens they'll be home before the wild-flower festival in May."

Cass was reaching for another slice of bread. "Didn't they know anyone local? Someone with experience?"

"Only the stinker who cornered me in the shed," Laurel shrugged, wrinkling her brow. "Rob said he didn't trust Frank with the money, but I'm sure he never figured he couldn't trust him with me. We were supposed to work together."

"Is your friend Rob blind?" Cass queried with a sly smile.

Cute, Cassidy, real cute, she thought wryly. I get

rid of Attila the Hun and he's replaced with a comedian. Granted, he had given her a compliment, but she'd been trying to tell a serious story, and he kept reducing it to one-liners.

Laurel shoved a lunchmeat package at him again. "You'd better have some salami. You're already too full of baloney, Mr. Cassidy."

Concentrating on his plate, Cass asked her to go on.

"There's not much more," Laurel sighed flatly. "I'm here in Julian for the next month—almost—and I have no idea how I'm going to keep their store running smoothly."

"Frank quit?" Cass asked.

"I fired him," she answered. "I really had no choice, but it's a heck of a dilemma. He threatened to kill Bear." There. That should make him see the situation in a more serious light, she thought.

Eyebrows raised, Cass nodded, then went on to make short work of his remaining lunch and open one of the cartons of orange juice Laurel had provided.

The phone rang. Stepping quickly over to the instrument on the wall, Laurel cheerfully answered, "Rob's Market." Then a stricken expression crept across her pale skin, and she fell silent.

Hauntingly, the male voice filled her ear with ugly threats. A combination of rage and fear flowed through Laurel in ever-increasing waves, leaving her body weak and trembling. Bright color coursed back into her cheeks. Frank wasn't going to get away with threatening her—not her. He would find out that Laurel Phillips was not someone to trifle with. And she was *not* going to listen to one more word from his filthy mouth.

From his vantage point, Cass could see her hand shake as she slammed the receiver back into its cradle. Quietly, he watched with concern as she returned to her perch on the cases of canned goods, her fury continuing to mount. "That skunk!" she said furiously.

Fighting the instinct to put his arm around her shoulders, Cass simply asked, "The lecher?"

Laurel nodded affirmatively.

"What did he say?" Cass pressed, his deep, gentle voice beginning to crackle with shared hostility.

"I—I don't want to repeat it," Laurel stammered. "It was awful."

Cass leaned back against the pile of boxes behind him, took a deep breath, and released it with an audible woosh. "What will you do?" He queried softly.

Shaking her head from side to side, Laurel shrugged. "I don't know, yet, but I'll think of something," she answered, pressing her lips into a thin line.

"You're a very cool cucumber, Ms. Phillips," Cass observed. "Very calm and collected."

"Thank you," she said, taking his opinions as a compliment, "I've always been able to handle the situations in my life by using my head and reasoning it out." The jangle of the phone behind her sent Laurel jumping off the crate. She stood transfixed, her arm barely extended toward the ringing telephone, as Cass brushed past her to yank the receiver off the wall and lift it to his ear.

His blue eyes deepened and snapped with electricity under furrowed brows as he listened to the man on the other end of the line. Finally, he had heard enough. "Now, now," Cass said sarcastically, "is that any way to talk to a lady?"

Laurel couldn't hear Frank, but it was easy enough to guess the slant of the conversation. She had heard a portion of it only minutes before.

"None of your business, scum," Cass spat into the phone.

Sitting back down, Laurel listened in fascination as the man took over where his dog had left off. The exchange was interesting, but unnecessary. She could have handled Frank if Cass had given her a few seconds to pull herself together.

"Listen," Cass said angrily, "stop bothering the lady, or you'll have to answer to me. She's not alone anymore, and I intend to see that she's protected." A scowl crossed his face and anger blazed in his eyes. "You're damn right, scum," he spat, "I'm staying—as long as she needs me!"

"Hey, wait a minute!" Laurel jumped to her feet. "I can take care of myself."

Cass clamped his broad hand over the mouthpiece. "I know, I know," he hissed. "Now shut up, will you?"

With her teeth clenched tightly together, Laurel sat rigidly on the boxes. How dare he tell her to shut up? Who did he think he was, some knight in shining armor, or some avenging angel who went around rescuing people? Well, not her, thank you. She didn't need him or anyone, and, Laurel proudly reminded herself, she never had.

WINTER'S PROMISE

Ending the confrontation on the phone with a terse, "Buzz off," Cass slammed down the receiver. "Now," he said to the fuming Laurel, "what's *your* problem?"

"Problem?" she snapped, "First him and now you, that's my problem. I told you, I can take care of myself. There's no need for you to stay. I don't need protecting. Do I make myself clear?"

"Quite."

"In that case, I suggest you make plans to leave," she said, pointing a quivering finger toward the door. He had mooched one free meal and obviously liked it enough to try for more. Well, she was nobody's fool. He wasn't going to get away with it.

Cass snorted a chuckle. "Never fear, milady, I have no intention of staying."

"But you told Frank—"

"I know. Don't get excited. I intend to phone the police, apprise them of your predicament, then fade off into the sunset with my faithful dog."

"Oh," she said, beginning to lose her anger and relax. That was using his head. He must be fairly intelligent, in spite of his choice of life-style. I wonder what possesses a man like that to take to the road? She decided to ask. After all, he already knew more about her than most people she had known for some time. "Tell me," she probed, "what made you choose to live as you do?"

A wry smile twisted the firm lips beneath the neatly trimmed mustache. "It was Bear's idea."

"Oh, come on, I'm serious," she insisted. "Don't you have a home, or a wife, or someone?" Laurel would have seen she had touched a nerve, even if she hadn't been a trained psychologist.

Cass stiffened. "No." He turned to the phone, dialed the operator, and asked for the police. When he had hung up the receiver, he faced Laurel apologetically. "Sorry," he said, sitting on the edge of a pile of cases, "no dice."

"What did they say?" she asked incredulously.

"Well, it seems threats without proof of violence don't warrant much action. They offered to drive by the store and your house once in a while," he concluded dryly.

"That's all?"

"That's all," he said with resignation. "I guess I'll have to stay the night, after all."

"Oh no, you don't," Laurel snapped, "The free ride is over."

His expression hardened. "Is that what you think?"

"Yes," she answered coldly, her jaw set.

"I'll bet if I were dressed in a silk suit and tie, you'd be more than glad for me to stay," he countered. "Well?"

"Mr. Cassidy, I don't need anyone," Laurel insisted, squaring her shoulders. "Silk suit or blue jeans notwithstanding, I told you, I can take care of myself."

"Like in the shed?" he asked pointedly.

"You needn't rub it in."

"But *you* need to remember it," Cass said. "Remember how you felt and what you thought he was going to do, then picture it happening again."

"Stop it!"

"No, you stop it. Stop insisting how liberated you are and use your head."

She glared at him.

"I'll concede your female rights," he went on, "but you'd better be prepared to admit that a man, almost any man, is stronger than you. In a contest of brute strength, who'd win?"

"I have my mind, my wits."

"And where does it say that Frank will listen?" Cass asked stiffly.

She shivered. Raising her eyes to meet his st[eady] gaze, she inquired seriously, "Want to sell your

"What, and break up a perfect team of m[an and] beast?" he laughed. "Sorry. Besides, Bear is a p[urebred] Newf—a Newfoundland—not a mutt. He wouldn't come cheap."

"Where in the world did *you* get him, then?" she asked, still defensive.

"Perhaps, Ms. Phillips, I was not always a wanderer," he said crisply. "Now to get back to your current problem. I'm not about to abandon you to this Frank character, at least not after I told him I'd be staying. You may ask us to curl up in your yard if you wish, but Bear and I are spending the night."

She felt there must be another way. Accepting a man's protection was foreign to her. She was independent, self-sufficient, capable, and, unfortunately, more alone than she had ever been in her life. Laurel reminded herself of all this with resignation.

She had to admit that Cass's way was best.

"Okay," she told him. "Mr. Cassidy and friend are invited to stay the night, but that's all, so don't get any wrong ideas. The store closes at six, and I'll be tied up until then. Do you want to wait back here?"

He stretched, yawning. "No thanks. I think I'll walk around and see the sights. I understand there are some old gold mines close by, and I spotted a museum down the hill. I had intended to see that on my way through town," he continued, "but Bear had other plans." Smiling slightly, he swung the pack to one shoulder. "See you later."

Watching him leave, Laurel was surprised to find herself sorry to see him go. He had made her angry, but he had seemed to have her best interests at heart. That alone was rare. In the cutthroat world of the big city, few people looked out for others. They were too busy trying to survive themselves. This small-town atmosphere was going to take some getting used to, and so was a man named Cassidy. She shrugged. He couldn't be for real, not the way she saw him. He had to have ulterior motives. It was just a matter of exposing them.

Sandy tried, halfheartedly, to provide a solution to Laurel's problems. As a recent bride, the young cashier didn't want her new boss as a house guest, yet felt compelled to offer. "Really, Laurel," Sandy said, "we can make room. It's a small place, but—"

"No, no," Laurel interrupted. "You and Jim don't need me underfoot. Besides, I prefer to be on my own, to do whatever I want. After all, I live alone in Ohio with no difficulty."

"Yes, but you said there were doormen and guards in your apartment building," Sandy reminded her.

"True," Laurel smiled, "but I'm sure I'm normally in more danger just crossing the street in downtown Cleveland. Frank makes a lot of macho noises, but I don't expect to see him again."

"I hope you're right," Sandy added.

"I'm right." Laurel smiled to herself. She could honestly say that her judgment was extremely reliable. It might not sound very humble, but Laurel Phillips was almost always right and proud of it.

"Listen, Sandy," she went on, "it's late. Why don't you run on home to your husband? Dave has already left, and I'll close up. I need to get a few groceries for myself before I leave."

"Are you sure?" the girl asked slowly. "Will you be safe?"

"Of course. Now, scoot." Opening the door for Sandy, Laurel made sure the sign read CLOSED before she locked herself in. "I suppose I'll have to feed him again," she murmured, thinking of Cass. He's done it, all right. One more free meal, coming up, for the moocher and his dog.

Bagging her groceries, Laurel set them on the counter and closed out the cash register, relieved when the totals balanced on the first try.

After pulling on her coat and hat, she swept the bag into one arm, fitted her key into the lock, and stepped outside. Cass would be there, would walk her home, and she'd invite him for dinner. What else could she do?

A chilly wind rippled the fine strands of auburn hair peeking out from under her hat. She looked around, temporarily blinded by the bright sun shining over the hip of a ridge to the west. Where was he? Drat him. He'd left her, just like the drifter he was. I should have known, she thought. People like him were no good, unreliable, shiftless . . .

A warm, furry, black shape leaned lazily against her legs. Bear! Pocketing her keys, she thankfully patted the broad head with her free hand.

"Here, let me get that," Cass said quietly, his voice reminding her of rippling velvet.

Laurel pivoted. He stood close, so very close, as he lifted the heavy bag from her arms. A strange, internal stirring was unsettling her. The physical reaction was akin to fear, yet she felt drawn to Cass rather than repulsed. All she had to do was lean a little to her right and she would be in his arms. Laurel stopped herself, her heart beginning to pound, her breathing becoming irrationally ragged. Good grief! Even men she had dated on a more or less regular basis hadn't caused her emotions and imagination to run away with her like this.

Cass had his pack on his back, a down jacket covering his blue plaid shirt, and a knitted cap pulled down over his hair.

"I can handle it," she stammered quickly. "You have your pack and my hands are empty."

He shrugged, releasing the sack. "Have it your way. Which way is home?"

Pointing up a fairly steep hill, Laurel replied, "One block on the right."

Falling into step beside her, Cass glanced at Laurel, his clear blue eyes crinkling at the corners as a small smile curled his mustache. "Do you always dress like that?" he asked.

"What do you mean?" Laurel was proud of her woolen jacket and perky hat. The muted browns elegantly matched her basic brown and beige wardrobe. Her shoes matched, too, so what could he be alluding to?

"Oh, nothing," Cass responded. "It's just that jeans and wool socks seem far more sensible here in the mountains. Aren't you freezing? There's not enough leather in those shoes to keep a flea warm."

Bluntness seemed to be the man's forte, she grumbled to herself. He'd do well to control his words in a more civilized manner and not be so critical of others. It didn't matter to Laurel that Cass was right; it was simply in poor taste to speak so honestly.

"I'm fine," Laurel fibbed. In truth, her feet were killing her from standing all day. Most of her clothes and shoes were far better suited to her usual desk job, and Laurel had long ago decided, from the aches in her body, that she was, too.

Trudging up the last few yards of the uneven dirt path, she suddenly recalled something Cass had said, something that her mind refused to bury in the depths of her subconscious. Fleas? Fleas. Oh, dear, now what? This wasn't even her house, and Laurel had been considering taking in a dog and a drifter, both of whom might very well be infested with all sorts of creepy crawlies. It would be impolite to ask, but what else could she do? She'd just have to be especially tactful. Surely, Cass would understand. After all, he seemed to be an expert at speaking *his* mind.

They climbed the stone steps to the concrete porch, and Laurel inserted her key in the heavy wooden door. "Uh, Mr. Cassidy," she began hesitantly, then lost her nerve.

"Yes?" he asked.

"Oh, ah, well, I just wondered if you like pizza."

"As a matter of fact, I do," he said. "Is that an invitation to dinner?"

"Of course," Laurel conceded, "But—"

"Good," Cass interrupted with slightly chattering teeth. "Then don't you think we should go in? In case you haven't noticed, it's freezing out here."

"Well, yes, but," Laurel stammered. "Oh, drat," she said, plunging through the door, "Come on. We can talk in here."

"Bear, too?" Cass asked, nodding toward the placidly waiting dog.

"Why not?" Laurel muttered, thoroughly disgusted with herself. "At least *he's* wearing a flea collar—I hope."

Chapter Three

&

Laurel flicked on the overhead light, illuminating the small, cozy living room and kitchen area, then took her bag of groceries to the counter by the sink. After adjusting the bag to keep it from falling, she turned back to her guests. She had to ask, and soon.

Standing in the middle of the living room, Cass was gazing appreciatively at the warmly decorated room as he removed his coat and hat. He sensed Laurel's eyes on him. "It has a homey air, don't you think?" he asked politely. "I like Early American. It's down to earth."

"I guess so," she replied. "Listen, Mr. Cassidy, I—I have to ask you something. Please don't be offended," she continued, "but this is not my house, and, well, I have a certain responsibility to my friends. Do you understand?"

"Not one word," he said, shaking his head. "Would you like to try again?"

"Well, to put it delicately," Laurel said softly, "is, is Bear likely to be, ah, buggy? You know, fleas?"

"No," Cass answered clearly. "He wears a flea collar. Anything else?"

There was no avoiding it. Still, her question came out with all the finesse of a runaway freight train. "And you, Mr. Cassidy? Do you have one too?"

Perhaps it was the slight tremor in her voice, perhaps the widening of her golden hazel eyes, or perhaps it was the question itself. Regardless, John Cassidy placed both fists on his hips, leaned back, and roared with laughter.

"What's so funny?" Laurel demanded.

"You!" Cass said between gales of laughter. "I thought it—it was—*me*—you were scared of."

"Well, hardly," Laurel insisted. She wasn't afraid of him—attracted, maybe, but not afraid. It was her own reactions that frightened her, but Laurel knew she could keep those in check.

Reflecting the gay atmosphere, Bear wagged his tail, galloping merrily around the room.

His mirth doubled Cass over as he hugged his sides, trying to suppress his laughter. "I—I'm sorry, Laurel, honestly," he finally managed to say, "but you're too much."

"Thanks a heap," she said dryly. He had tried to distract her and he wasn't going to get away with it. "Well, Cassidy," she pressed, "I'm waiting. Are you buggy or not?"

"Would you recognize a problem if you saw one?" he chuckled.

"My brother brought an awful case home from camp one year," she explained.

He crossed the room. Taking her hands in his,

Cass dropped to one knee in front of her and placed her hands on the crown of his head. "Okay, see for yourself."

Laurel recoiled from the unexpected contact.

"Really, Mr. Cassidy," she said formally, "that won't be necessary. I'm perfectly willing to take your word for it."

"Well, I'm not," he insisted. "Suppose you find something in the house after I'm gone? Who'll get the blame? Me. Now look, or I'll spend the evening kneeling at your feet."

"You wouldn't."

"Oh, yes, I would," he said forcefully.

"But—but, I know this must be embarrassing to you," Laurel apologized.

"Hah! Not nearly as embarrassing as it'll be if you find something. Please, get it over with, Ms. Phillips. This position isn't easy on the knee."

Laurel agreed reluctantly and began to work her slim fingers through his soft, silky, brown hair. As it fell gently over her hands, she was more than surprised to find it so clean, so thick, and so obviously well cared for.

Touching him was a pleasurable experience, so much so that Laurel probed for longer than was really necessary before she tapped him on the shoulder. "I'm finished," she announced. "You pass."

He stood up before her, reaching slowly to grasp her wrists. "No. You're not done yet," he said quietly, placing her palms against his face and drawing her smaller hands over his beard.

The contact was unnerving. This hair felt so

different, much more coarse and curly, and so warm. Wide-eyed, Laurel stared at his face: the sandy brown beard and mustache outlining his firm lips; a strong, straight nose; twinkling blue eyes, decorated at the corners with the fine lines from a thousand broad smiles; straight brows; and the soft, shiny hair she had so recently mussed. The greenish gold of her eyes misted as she let her gaze travel over him, coming to rest in the depths of his own gentle eyes.

Cass hadn't moved. His large hands were still cupped over hers, holding them tenderly against his face. "You're right," he said finally in a husky voice, "that's enough. It's a good thing for both of us we don't find each other attractive." He turned to the fireplace. "You get dinner and I'll make a fire. How about it?"

"Sounds fair," she said quietly, still wrapped up in the spell of his touch. Watching him stack the logs and strike a match, Laurel was amazed at the way he fit so perfectly in the little house. He seemed far more in keeping with the surroundings than Laurel did. The soft plaid of his shirt blended beautifully with the colorful braided rug and Colonial tweed couch, all of them reflecting a homespun quality. But, there was more to it than that. Cass seemed to exude the same all-encompassing warmth Laurel had felt when she first entered Joan and Rob's home. How strange that a man like that—oh well, he would be gone in the morning, and that would be the end of it.

Turning her attention to the pizza, Laurel piled the

cheese and sliced pepperoni generously over the thick, tomato-laden sauce, then opened a can of mushrooms.

Perched on the raised, stone hearth, Cass was staring silently into the leaping flames, seemingly lost in thought. Laurel hated to disturb him. Still, if he didn't like mushrooms she didn't want to add them. He might be uncultured, but he was her guest.

With the open can in one hand, she crossed the room. Placing her other hand on his shoulder, Laurel felt him flinch slightly. "Cass?"

"I think Bear and I should stay outside tonight," he said.

"We can discuss that later," she replied, matter-of-factly. "Right now, I need to know if you like mushrooms."

Cassidy let his eyes travel to her face as he shifted his weight to look at her. "Yes, Ms. Phillips," he said with a mellow, almost tender intonation. "If you do, I do."

What a strange thing for him to say. Laurel could sense his eyes following her as she returned to the kitchen, but it wasn't an insidiously raking stare like Frank's. It felt more like a form of affection, coupled with a remote kind of sadness.

Dinner relaxed them both. Only one piece of pizza remained on the round, aluminum tray. Flinging herself back against the overstuffed cushions of the couch, Laurel complained loudly.

"Ooh! Am I stuffed. I feel like a kid after Thanksgiving dinner. I ate too much."

Cass stood and stretched. "Does that mean Bear can have the last piece?"

"Sure. Unless you want to save it for the road tomorrow."

"No thanks," he replied, shaking his head. "If I ate like this all the time, I couldn't even walk let alone carry my pack."

"Then I take it you don't want ice cream for dessert," Laurel said, beginning to smile.

"Tell you what," he said, rummaging through a compartment in his pack, "how about these for dessert?"

"Apples?" Laurel eyed the shiny, red fruit. "Could I save mine? I really am full."

Cass placed the two apples together on the coffee table then sank into a broad, comfortable chair across from her. "Sure, it'll give you something to remember me by," he said placidly.

"Somehow, I think I'll remember you for some time to come. You're a very unusual person, Cass."

"So are you," he countered. "Tell me, what are your life's goals, Laurel? Any special plans?"

Laurel slipped off her shoes and propped her tired feet on the coffee table. "Well, I'm halfway to my Ph.D. That's the next step. Then, who knows?"

"That's the trouble with some kinds of goals," he mused, tucking his hands behind his head and leaning back. "Once you've attained them, there's nowhere else to go. Now, if your objectives were happiness, or a better understanding of yourself or the universe, then you could keep striving toward them and grow at the same time."

"Like chasing rainbows? No thanks," she said firmly. "I know for a fact that those are unattainable."

"You sound very sure."

"I am. I used to consider such possibilities, but now I see them for what they are—sheer folly."

"I don't suppose you take much time out for fun, then, do you?" he asked.

"Fun? Of course I do," Laurel responded. "Not that it's any business of yours. But my studies and job take up a great deal of my time. Besides, they're fun."

"I'll wager they take up all your time," Cass observed, leaning forward with his elbows on his knees, his hands clasped between them. "Where did you go on your last vacation?"

"Oh, well, I haven't felt the need to take a vacation for a while," she explained. "As it has turned out, I needed the accumulated time to use here." Laurel swept her arm around the warmly glowing room.

Cass walked to the hearth, added another log, and probed the coals with the poker. "Won't you be missed at home?"

"You mean my family?" Laurel asked dryly.

"That," he replied, "or perhaps a man, a boyfriend."

"No," she snorted, "I haven't found a man who fits my ideals."

Slipping his hands into the pockets of his jeans, Cass leaned against the stone mantel. "Which are?" he asked.

Perhaps, Laurel thought, if she told him he'd quit asking such personal questions. She tilted her head back and closed her eyes. "Well, he should be accomplished. You know—a good education, sensible goals and the means to achieve them. He should be stable, socially acceptable, and from a good family." She hesitated, opening her eyes. "I guess that's all."

"You're sure?" he asked pensively.

Nodding, Laurel furrowed her brow, trying to read the puzzling expression on Cass's face.

Thoughtfully, he drew his hand over his beard, closing his fingers at the point of his chin. "I think you've forgotten a few necessary elements," he drawled. "Like loving and caring, tenderness and affection, enjoying each other's company, having fun, becoming better people for having been together." He paused. "Things like that, Laurel."

Having a wandering vagabond lecture her was the last straw. Enough was enough. "No dice, Mr. Cassidy. Those lofty ideals may be fine for you, but they have no bearing on my life. I'm a very practical person." Now, it was her turn to ask the questions. "What brings you to Julian?"

Cass shrugged his shoulders. "I told you. It was all Bear's idea."

"Sure," she gibed, "but he's not talking, so let's start with your family."

"Midwest," he said succinctly.

"And out here?" she pressed. "No attachments?"

"Not anymore," he responded, his voice hauntingly hollow.

"You were close to someone once?" Laurel probed, suddenly aware that she'd touched the edge of a painful truth.

Cass snorted and plunked his bulk down into the chair. "I don't really know, anymore," he said honestly.

"What I wanted and what Elizabeth wanted weren't the same things."

"Just like you and me," she observed.

"No, I don't think so," Cass said slowly. "I think, if we gave ourselves time and a reasonable chance to get to know each other, you and I might find we're similar."

"*Us?* You must be joking," Laurel squeaked. What a totally ridiculous conception. Imagine her, a professional psychologist with a stack of degrees to her credit, and him, a worthless drifter. If he didn't seem so serious, she might have laughed aloud.

Without a reply, Cass rose, slipped into his jacket, and reached for his pack. "Come on, Bear, it's time to go." The big dog peeled open one brown eye, obviously not thrilled about the idea of leaving the warm hearth.

"But—but, it's freezing out there!" Laurel protested. "Really, I don't mind if you two sleep in here."

"I don't know, Laurel," he said. "If I stay inside the neighbors will have a field day with your reputation. Besides, we're used to roughing it."

Laurel brushed aside the beige eyelet curtains, peering through the frosty windowpanes. "You're crazy, Cass. Surely you don't sleep out in weather like this all the time, do you?"

Cass shrugged. "Yes and no. When the temperature drops, I usually pitch my tent at dusk and settle down before the chill sets in. That way, we're warm and dry all night."

"And now?" Laurel reasoned. "Now you'll freeze to death or catch pneumonia. Uh uh, not on my doorstep you don't!" She flounced boldly across the room, seeming even shorter in her bare feet, and glared up at Cass's broad frame. "I insist. It will be quite proper for you to sleep in here, and I'll lock my bedroom door."

Ironic humor shone in his blue eyes. "You're a brave little thing, aren't you?" he asked, placing his hands gently on her shoulders. "You're going to lock your door, when we've been here—together—all evening, and I could have had my way with you any time."

Widening beneath her sweeping lashes, Laurel's hazel eyes stared incredulously at him. He was bigger than she, obviously much stronger, and even more obviously, very male. He could have, but he didn't, and he wouldn't. Somehow, even after he had placed the idea in her mind Laurel knew she was safe with him. "I—I don't know why," she said hesitantly, her chin thrust high, "but I trust you completely."

A benevolent smile curled his lips. "You should, Laurel," he said in a tender, quiet tone. "You're really very lovely, but . . ."

"Not your type, I'll bet," she interrupted.

"No one is, right now," he explained. "Perhaps, if we'd met another time . . ."

Or in another world, she thought. My world. Why couldn't you be a professional man, Cass? Why couldn't you have lived in Cleveland so I'd be going back to you at the end of this whole episode? And why am I standing here enjoying the touch of your hands like some schoolgirl with her first crush?

Seconds passed before Laurel regained her cool reserve and headed for her bedroom. "The bathroom is through there," she said, pointing across the room. "I'll give you a few minutes, then use it myself. Good night, Mr. Cassidy."

His warm, appealing voice wrapped around her. "Good night, Laurel."

When she had returned from the bathroom, Cass was snuggled into his sleeping bag on the living room floor, while Bear had chosen to sleep beside Laurel. "Well, old boy, I guess your half of the team is welcome here," she said, patting his silky fur, "but don't disturb me before morning. I'm beat."

She was. Still, in spite of her exhaustion, Laurel lay staring at the ceiling, waiting for the sleep that eluded her. A rather fuzzy image swam in front of her eyes when she closed them, and Laurel giggled. Fuzzy was right. Clamping her hand over her mouth to stifle the noise, she remembered how silly Cass had looked when she had parted his hair. And that beard, how odd it had felt to her sensitive fingers. *I wonder what it would feel like on my cheek—or my lips,* she thought absently.

Laughter vanished as she realized that she had just been thinking about kissing him, of all things. She tucked the covers more tightly around her. He was attractive, in a rough sort of way, almost the way she had envisioned the early settlers of the West. But *Laurel Phillips is no pioneer's lady,* she reminded herself. The man she'd choose would be refined, cultured, and well educated, a man she would be proud to show off. Her giggles returned. Wouldn't her colleagues have fun gossiping if she and Cass . . . That was impossible, of course, but harmless to fantasize about. Imagine having those strong arms around her, that bearded face bending to hers.

This time, when Laurel closed her eyes, she welcomed thoughts of Cass. Why not? He'd be gone in the morning.

Laurel's eyes snapped open, her heart beating wildly. Peering into the blackness, she had only a split second to wonder what had awakened her when she heard the noise again. Bear was growling, a low and rumbling sound and his dark shadow was facing the door. She listened intently, holding her breath. Someone was moving stealthily about in the house. Perhaps Cass had gotten hungry or thirsty, she thought, perhaps . . . No. Bear would know his master's footfalls and accept them as normal.

The growl continued as the huge dog moved purposefully toward the door. If Laurel kept it closed, the dog would protect her. Surely, no one would attempt anything against her with her enormous guardian. She was safe, and—Cass! He was still in there with whoever was upsetting Bear. Laurel had Cass's dog for protection, but that left him alone and unaware. If he were in a deep sleep, he might not hear someone approach. Admittedly, he was strong, but asleep he could be overcome without fair warning.

Laurel listened. It was quiet. Nothing stirred in the little house. In two steps, she could be around the corner to check on Cass. If he were sleeping peacefully, there would be no need to disturb him. She was probably being silly, getting excited over a dog's growl. Her rapid heartbeat began to return to normal.

Slipping quietly out of bed, she pulled a fluffy, white robe over her long gown, knotted the sash, and stole across the room. Bear was way ahead of her, his nose pressed to the crack between the door and the jamb. The brass knob felt cold beneath her hand as she grasped it, twisting it slowly. Laurel wedged her body against the narrow opening, displacing the anxious dog. "Not yet, Bear," she whispered. "Let me take a peek first."

Opening the door only wide enough to squeeze through, she restrained the Newfoundland with her outstretched hand. "No, boy. Stay in there for a second."

Obediently, the animal waited, poised by the slightly open door.

That would be safe enough, Laurel thought. If she needed Bear, he could simply nose open the door the rest of the way and let himself out. Cautiously, Laurel padded to the corner of the door frame leading to the living room and peered into the dark room. A soft glow from the dying fire barely illuminated the center of the rug, but she could see and hear Cass snoring contentedly in his sleeping bag. All was well. Laurel sighed disgustedly. She had been acting like a total fool. Her feet were cold, she was tired, and she had crawled out of a warm bed to check on a grown man who could easily take care of himself. "Oh, well," she whispered, referring to herself with resignation, "some people have very vivid imaginations."

Laurel tensed suddenly. Someone was close to her—a presence felt rather than seen. As she spun around she saw a man's hand reaching for her. Realizing he'd been discovered, he lunged for the now terrified and vulnerable Laurel.

Her reflexes needed only a split second to act, and act they did. She ducked. Her robe was grabbed from behind. Screaming, Laurel struggled to shed it. Bear crashed against the door, but he miscalculated its opening and only succeeded in closing in firmly. Stuck inside Laurel's bedroom, the dog began to howl as if he were trying to break down the separation between them. The commotion was deafening.

With a shout of triumph, Laurel broke free of her robe, leaving it in a heap where the intruder had stood. The unfamiliar room became a jumble of obstacles as she dodged the furniture in her wild flight.

The phone. She must summon help. This could never have happened in her well-guarded apartment in Cleveland. Disoriented, Laurel lunged for the kitchen, tripping soundly over the large mass on the floor that had been the sleeping Cass. Strong arms wrapped tightly around her, enclosing Laurel in an inescapable embrace.

Fight. She knew she couldn't stand there and allow herself to be overcome. If she was going to be hurt, so was the person who had grabbed her. Her arms were pinned to her sides, but her legs were still free. Squirming and kicking violently, Laurel inflicted as much punishment on her attacker as she could before the pain in her toes insisted she stop. Someone was calling her name—someone who sounded far off.

Dragging his burden to the table by the couch, Cass reached quickly and flicked on the lamp. "Hey! Stop it, Laurel," he ordered. "It's okay. It's me. *It's me!*"

Laurel's breath froze in her throat, stifling her scream. She blinked furiously, trying to get her bearings. "Ah," she gasped in relief, folding herself willingly into his arms. "Thank God."

Holding her close, Cass let her catch her breath. With her cheek pressed reassuringly to his chest, he stroked her hair, calming her gently. "Are you okay?" he asked tenderly.

Laurel nodded, rubbing her face against him. He felt so good, so much like a safe haven in a raging storm, she wished she could stop time and remain in his arms forever.

Cass held her out at arm's length, tilting up her chin with one hand. "Are you sure?" he persisted. "You scared the hell out of me."

"You!" Laurel gasped. "You? What about me?" How like a man to think only of himself.

"Calm down and tell me what happened. All I know is, I was sound asleep when suddenly bedlam broke loose and you stomped me flat then kicked me black and blue."

"Serves you right for grabbing me like that," she retorted sharply. All Laurel really wanted was to be tucked back into Cass's arms, but she dared not ask. What would he think? Her eyes traveled over his solid torso. "Oh!" she gasped, forgetting her momentary anger. "You're not dressed."

His underwear covered him more than adequately, but left no doubt that he was very much a man. "I seldom sleep in my clothes," he snapped, aware of her intimate perusal of his physique. "If I put my pants on, will you please tell me what happened?"

She nodded affirmatively, her eyes glued to his powerful body. He had been sensually perplexing with his clothes *on*, but like this he was taking her breath away. Turning his back, Cass stepped into his jeans. As the denim covered his muscular legs, Laurel's memory continued to visualize the firm muscles and the fine, curling hairs covering them. She licked her lips nervously, cursing her vivid imagination as it suggested to her body how those hips and thighs might feel pressed against hers.

Cass spied her discarded robe and retrieved it for her, draping it over her shoulders. "Here. If I have to be dressed, so do you," he chided. "Besides, it will make it easier for me to concentrate on your story."

A slow, crimson flush crept to her cheeks. It was as if he had read her innermost thoughts.

Cass grinned. "That color goes well with your hair. You should blush all the time."

"Unfortunately, I do," she said, conscious of his arm still curved around her. "Do you think the intruder is gone?"

"Intruder? Damn it, woman, why didn't you *say* so?" he boomed. "I thought you'd had a nightmare or something." Leaving her shivering in the living room, Cass armed himself with the fireplace poker, freed his frantic dog from the confines of Laurel's bedroom, and began to search the house room by room.

Being alone, even though the area was lighted, wasn't Laurel's idea of safety. For her, safety under the present circumstances was a bearded man and a big, black dog. Distressingly, they had both temporarily left her, an oversight that could be remedied easily if she chose to follow them. She did. Coming up behind Cass, she was almost the recipient of a knock on the head with the poker. "Hey!" she shrieked, fending off the quickly checked blow.

"What are you doing here?" he hissed.

"I live here!" she exclaimed. "Besides, you and Bear left me, and I figured there was more safety in numbers. You make a lot of protective noises, but you abandoned me when I needed you most."

"You're right. I'm sorry." He took her by the hand. "Come on, but stay behind me."

It didn't take much coaxing to convince Laurel to do as he said. Being near his quiet strength buoyed her spirits. She didn't give him a chance to change his mind about letting her tag along, falling quickly into step behind him.

They found a window in the back porch that had been forced.

"There," Cass said as he locked it. "We know there's no one in the house now, and this will settle it."

"You're sure?" she murmured.

"Positive. We've covered every room and so has Bear. No stranger would get by his nose, even if we happened to miss seeing someone." Cass squeezed Laurel's hand. "You're safe."

"Thanks," she said gratefully. "How about a cup of coffee or hot chocolate? I need to sit down. I think the whole thing is beginning to hit me."

Guiding her to the kitchen, Cass offered her a chair at the breakfast bar and put on the tea kettle. "Sit, lady," he ordered affectionately. "I'm sure your feet are killing you, too, judging from the job you did on my shins."

"I—I'm really sorry," Laurel said. "Did I hurt you badly?"

"Well, you sure didn't help my hiking prowess."

"Oh, dear," she sighed innocently. "Is there anything I can do to make amends?"

A look of masculine humor flashed across Cass's rugged face, but he held back the first reply that occurred to him. This was definitely not *that* kind of lady. And he wasn't ready for any change in their relationship. "No, but thanks," he said seriously. "Now, tell me what happened—from the beginning."

While she finished her story, Cass poured boiling water into the two mugs of cocoa mix and placed one on the counter for Laurel. Cradling his own drink, he leaned languidly back against the counter top. "So, you didn't see who it was," he added.

"No, but I can guess."

"Mm hmm, so can I," Cass said thoughtfully. "Maybe now we can get you some police protection."

"How? Neither of us actually saw who it was. I'm still stuck," Laurel chimed in with sarcasm. "They won't believe us."

Cass took a deep breath, gazing fondly at the pretty figure huddled over her steaming mug. She was feisty, that was true, but no match, physically, for Frank. There was only one thing to do. "I think I'd better plan to stay a little while longer," he concluded aloud.

Her eyes darted sharply to his face. "What?"

"I can't very well abandon you now, can I?"

"What am I, a sinking ship?" she asked.

"No. You're more like a wild rose—beautiful but thorny."

Laurel cooled slightly. "Who appointed you my protector? Why should you care anyway? You don't even *know* me."

"I've asked myself the same questions, believe me," he replied. "It will only be until you can find a more suitable companion. I'm sure that when you look around someone else will fill the bill."

"Easily," she snapped. But would someone else? Laurel wondered. The way Cass had slipped into her life was a miracle in itself. Frank's horrible attack had somehow made her temporarily vulnerable, and Cass had stepped into the breach before she could rebuild her defenses.

She might be stubborn, but she wasn't a fool. The man was rather nice to have around and certainly personable once he got over his tendencies to try to control her. That part of their relationship, she knew she could handle. Physically, he wasn't at all hard to take, either. Laurel admitted her attraction to him, but she had never met a man who was irresistible, and she was sure Cass would be no exception.

Realistically, she couldn't allow him to stay without offering some type of compensation. After all, he would be missing out on other opportunities to earn survival money doing odd jobs. Perhaps . . . it certainly wouldn't hurt to ask. "Tell me," she began, "do you have any objections to working?"

Cass chuckled. "No. Why?"

"I was thinking. Since I've decided to accept your offer of temporary companionship, I feel I should reciprocate. You'll need money for your travels and I'll be shorthanded at the store."

He was smiling, sipping his cocoa.

"I couldn't pay much, but you and Bear could continue to eat with me. That would save you money. How about it?"

"If you're volunteering to feed that glutton," he said, pointing to his enormous dog, "how can I refuse? He'll make it worth my while in one day."

"Then it's settled," she said matter-of-factly. "You'll start tomorrow." Laurel glanced at the mantel clock. "Oops. I mean today. It's two A.M. Don't you think we'd better be getting back to bed?" Too late, she realized what she had said. "I—I mean . . ." Flustered, she fell silent.

"There's that lovely, rosy color again," Cass teased. "But you're right." He took the almost empty mug from her hands and placed it, together with his, in the sink. "We'll have the maid or the butler do the dishes in the morning," he quipped. "Good night, boss lady."

Laurel wrinkled up her nose. "Why don't you call me by my first name?" she suggested. "That boss lady title makes me feel funny."

"Okay . . . Laurel." He said her name slowly, almost sensuously.

She was instantly sorry that she had encouraged the continued familiarity. Her name seemed to roll off his lips like the intimate caress of a lover, sending tiny shocks of electricity up her spine. She sat, unmoving and speechless.

"Well," Cass said with a smile, reaching for the

waist of his jeans, "if you're not going to leave my bedroom, I guess I'll have to get undressed while you watch."

Her eyes grew wider, scanning his broad chest, narrow waist, and flat stomach. Drifting lower, her gaze fastened on his hands as he undid the button then reached for the zipper.

"Well?" he said crisply, hesitating.

"I'm going!" she sputtered as she jumped up. "I'm going." Bear trotted obediently after her, settling down next to the bed as Laurel tucked the covers tightly under her chin. The distressing events of the last twelve hours filled her mind until she began drifting off to sleep. Nothing had changed, she thought dreamily. Nothing except her unusual reactions to a friendly, bearded stranger with penetrating blue eyes and a warm, understanding smile that seemed to light up the whole room.

He had made, perhaps, a tiny, tiny chink in the impenetrable façade that was the professional Ms. Laurel Phillips.

Chapter Four

Tucking her head under the covers, Laurel sought to drown out the noise and deny the fact that morning had come. It was a futile effort. The neighbors must be—no. Fully awake, she realized where she was. There were no neighboring apartments with thin walls in Julian. But that noise!

She threw back the covers and, reaching for her robe, swung her feet to the floor. The sun was barely up, she noticed with disdain. Nights were short enough without prowlers taking up time that should be spent sleeping, and now this. Tying the sash of her robe, Laurel stomped to her bedroom door and jerked it open. Bear ducked out ahead of her, bounding like a puppy in search of a toy. Then the odor hit her. Egad! Bacon was sizzling amid the noise of a radio, playing some ridiculously loud song about cowboys and lost loves.

"What are you *doing*?" she demanded, holding her hands over her ears as she approached the kitchen like a vengeful god in search of a sacrifice. "Do you know what *time* it is?"

"Morning, sunshine," Cass chimed. "Ready for breakfast?"

"Ugh," Laurel groaned. She seated herself at the bar and put her head in her hands. "Don't you have a cup of coffee?"

He set a tall glass of bright orange liquid in front of her and went to let his dog out the front door.

"That's orange juice," she complained as he returned.

"Hey, you're very perceptive early in the morning," he said lightly. "It's good for you. Drink up."

Curling one side of her mouth in an imit[...] snarl, she lifted the glass to her lips and [...] cool sweetness. If this was a typical m[...] Cass, she was overjoyed their associatio[...] brief. "People who get up and head straight [...] kitchen are a pain," Laurel said.

"Ah, but I didn't," Cass replied. "I've already been out for a long walk."

"My hero," she snapped. "You were supposed to be guarding me."

Cass laughed. "Bear did as good a job as I could. Besides, you only keep me around because he and I are a pair. You always did like him best."

Ironically, he was partly right. Laurel had often missed the companionship that her mongrel dog had offered when she was growing up. There had been occasions when being with the animal were the only times she had felt loved and understood. Perhaps she would get herself a dog when she returned to Ohio. Something apartment sized, however. Too bad Newfs are so enormous, she thought, I'd sure like a dog like Bear. Speaking of which . . . Laurel went to the door in answer to the big dog's scratching and let him back in.

A voice on the radio rose in a plaintive crescendo. "And what do you call that?" Laurel grimaced, nodding toward the radio as she sat back down on the stool.

"Country music," he answered cheerfully. "You're lucky you can get the station so well up here in the mountains."

"Yeah. Lucky," Laurel winched as the voice repeated the wail.

"It grows on you," Cass teased.

"So does fungus if you let it," she replied flatly.

"I gather you don't care for my taste in music," he said, smiling and turning the sizzling strips of bacon with a fork. "I could switch it off."

Laurel rose from her chair. "Never mind. I'm going to go hide in the shower where I can't hear you or smell your culinary efforts. When I'm done, you can take a shower and get yourself cleaned up for work. Don't bother to save me any of that," she finished, gesturing toward the food.

"Okay, Mom," Cass promised. "Anything else?"

"Yes," she said, undaunted. "Make a pot of coffee, will you?"

"Your wish is my command, gracious lady." He bowed in her direction. "Anyone so beautiful, so agreeable, and so very cheerful in the morning deserves whatever she asks. Tomorrow, I'll just hand you a lemon for breakfast. It will suit your mood."

"Anyone who gets up with the sun, wakes everyone else, and insists on foisting food on unsuspecting victims should be run out of town on a rail," she countered. "Your bacon is burning," she said with some pleasure, as she turned and left the room.

The shower helped. By the time Laurel had towel dried her wavy hair and applied what little make-up she wore, she felt more human. Poor Cass. He had been trying to be helpful and she'd been less than gracious. She sighed, surveying her closet full of coordinated outfits. He'd been right about that, too, she mused. Her clothes were far more suitable for the office than for the market. Laurel wondered what she would look like in jeans. She knew she could get a pair at the dry goods store and wear them today, if she wanted, especially if she wore a sweater, or something equally adaptable. She chose a long-sleeved, ivory knit that fastened along one shoulder with tiny pearl buttons and tapered to a fitted waist. Her gabardine slacks could easily be replaced by blue jeans, she decided as she put on her shoes. "Oooh," Laurel moaned, "maybe sneakers, too. My feet are killing me." Slipping off the pumps, she carried them with her to the living room. Cassidy was busy doing the dishes. "Okay, Cass," she announced, "it's all yours."

A smile curled his mustache as he turned and looked her up and down. "What is?" he teased, waiting for the blush he knew his remarks would trigger. He wasn't disappointed. A warm glow rose to Laurel's cheeks.

Uncouth. Definitely uncouth. "The shower, Mr. Cassidy," she said stiffly, angry at her predictable reaction to his taunts. He started to open his mouth, but Laurel spoke first. "I know, I know, I'm a lovely color—again. Thanks to you."

"Me?" he said innocently. "What did I do?"

"Nothing," Laurel admitted ruefully. "There's just something about the way you ask a question, with that mischievous smile of yours, that seems to overstimulate my sensitive cardiovascular system," she said.

Cass chuckled. Drying his hands, he began poking through his pack for clean clothes. "That is the most clinical description of a lady's lovely blush that I've ever heard," he snickered. "I'd hate to hear you describe something as intimate as a kiss."

"Don't worry," she retorted. "Chances of that are nonexistent."

He was still laughing softly to himself when he closed the bathroom door and turned on the shower.

By the time Cass returned to the kitchen, Laurel had managed to add enough water to his coffee to make it almost palatable.

Furrowing his brow, Cass eyed the cup of dark liquid. "Was it all right?" he asked hesitantly.

Laurel snorted. "It is now," she said, but smiled at him to soften her derogatory tone.

"Uh oh, that's what I was afraid of. I'm not used to making coffee. There were no instructions, so I guessed."

"Oh," she said quietly, contemplating her cup.

"Awful?" he asked.

"The worst," she laughed, "but thanks for trying." Looking up at Cass, Laurel was surprised to find he didn't look any different from when she'd first met him—same twinkling blue eyes, same hair curling over his collar, same beard and mustache. He must not realize how late it was getting. "You'd better hurry, if you're going to be ready to leave with me," she prompted.

Cass shrugged, "I am ready."

"But you haven't shaved," she corrected.

"Yes, I have," he said, tilting back his head to display the clean-shaven neck under his beard. "See?"

"What I see," Laurel insisted, "is a man who looks like he just fell off a slow-moving freight. The beard will have to go."

"Over my dead body!" Cass exclaimed. "The beard is an integral part of me. No dice."

Laurel was flabergasted. "You can't mean you intend to go to work looking like, like—"

"Whoa!" Cass said. "I've been told by more than one beautiful lady that she found my beard an asset, especially in times of close—"

"Wait! I don't want to hear how other women love your furry face. Okay, the beard stays. Since you won't be working for me very long, I can hardly make it a hard and fast rule. Your hair could use a trim, though."

"What is it with you, Laurel?" he asked with a grin. "First you want to get your hands on my fuzzy dog, then my furry face, and now my hair. What you need, is a fuzzy, furry teddy bear to satisfy your cravings."

"Very funny," she said dryly. "I used to cut my brother's hair, and I'm really very good at it."

He hesitated, searching her steady, greenish-gold gaze. "Promise not to get carried away?"

Drawing her finger over her heart in the shape of an *X*, Laurel said, "Cross my heart. Sit down."

"And you won't drop itchy little pieces of hair down my shirt?" he added as Laurel draped a towel over his shoulders.

"Of course not," she drawled in a syrupy-sweet purr.

"I'm leaving," he announced, starting to rise.

Placing her hands on his shoulders, Laurel caught him off balance, toppling him back into the chair. "Sit," she ordered.

Cass finally relaxed as she carefully snipped his hair. "Tell me about your brother. What's his name?"

"The other kids always called him Baldy," Laurel said, unable to stifle the giggles she felt coming on when Cass wheeled to look at her in terror. "Relax, I was only kidding," she assured him. "His name is Steve, and he's been in the Air Force since I was a teenager. He says he likes it, so I suppose he'll make a career of it." She paused. "What about you, Cassidy? What are your plans for the future?"

He shrugged noncommittally. "Nothing special. One day at a time is the way I plan to take it for a while. Why?"

"No reason," Laurel said, continuing to snip at his hair, "except, you interest me as a psychologist."

"Your interest is purely professional, is that it?"

"Of course," she replied seriously.

"And Laurel, the woman, isn't the least bit curious?"

"There's no separation between me and my career.

WINTER'S PROMISE

I am, first and foremost, a professional person," she assured him.

"Always?"

"Always," she reiterated, unprepared for his sudden move.

Reaching back over his shoulder, he caught her wrist in one strong hand and pulled her down to his level, twisting his head to plant a firm kiss squarely on her lips. His beard tantalized the soft skin of her face, leaving a kind of raspy tingle when he released her.

"Stop that!" Laurel demanded. "What do you think you're doing?"

"Just testing," Cass said cynically. "You were right. That was definitely not a woman's kiss."

How dare he? "Humph. What makes you think I care about *your* opinions?" she snapped, wresting her arm free from his grip. She shook the scissors at him. "Now, shape up and hold still, or you'll be doing an impression of Van Gogh—*after* he cut off his ear."

"You're a *mean* woman, Ms. Phillips."

"And don't you forget it," she said as she sprinkled bits of hair into his collar. That would teach him not to fool with her. "There, I'm finished."

Cass wiggled his broad shoulders, feeling the offending wisps sliding down his back. He turned to Laurel, scowling. "Did you?" he demanded.

Giggling, Laurel clasped both hands over her mouth, tears of laughter beginning to gather in her eyes. "I—I'm sorry," she gasped between bursts of laughter. "I—I couldn't resist. Besides, you deserved it, after that crack about my kissing."

As Cass unbuttoned his shirt, tugging the tails out of his snug jeans, Laurel struggled to get a grip on her emotions. I'm just tense with all that's been happening, she reasoned, and laughter is the best release I could have chosen. But why, oh why, did I do that to him, especially after he kissed me?

"Okay, Ms. Phillips," Cass said forcefully, pulling his shirt off and shaking it out. "Dust!"

"What?"

"Get the hair off, or I'll dump a pile of it down your stubborn little neck," he threatened, turning his broad back to Laurel.

"You wouldn't."

"Don't bet on it," he warned. "Now brush me off."

Her hands slid lightly over the smooth warmth of his back, feeling the taut, rippling muscles lying just under the skin. Touching him was pleasing to her senses, and her fingers hesitated, savoring the feeling. Laurel's face still tingled from the momentary stroke of his beard on her cheeks and she could taste his kiss on her lips. He had barely given her time to realize she was being kissed, let alone begin to enjoy it or return it. Laurel felt the strange desire to nibble the baby-soft skin between his shoulder blades.

"Done?" he barked, a little too harshly.

"Uh—not quite," she lied, brushing her hands over his shoulders and down his arms in an overt caress. Whatever had possessed her to do that? Thank God she had fought the impulse to kiss his back!

Cass moved away. Turning his shirt right side out, he put it on. "That's fine. Thanks."

WINTER'S PROMISE

And why in the world had she continued to touch him, she wondered as her pulse raced. She hadn't needed to, and Laurel knew it. It was crazy—oops. How many times had professors told them not to use that word. Still, in a lay sense it fit. Was she becoming unbalanced? This vagabond had no rightful place in her present or her future. Then why did she find him so attractive, with his rough, masculine ways? And why, *why*, did the physical sensation of his taunting kiss linger so? He certainly wasn't like any other man she had ever known.

"Coming?" Cass asked, jolting her out of her reverie.

Reaching for her shoes, Laurel wedged her protesting toes into the sleek black pumps. Today was the day for sneakers, she decided at once. Enough suffering for Laurel Phillips. "Did you make sure everything was turned off in the kitchen?" she asked, pulling on her jacket. After all, Cass was used to campfires and the like.

"If there's anything turned on around here, Laurel, it's your fault," he grumbled.

Her eyes snapped up to meet his. Damn. Did it show? Was he feeling it, too? From his terse comment, it was fairly obvious he was. She'd have to be especially careful from now on, to avoid further incidents. Laurel thought back to his mocking kiss, the feel of his bare back, her unreasonable urge to kiss his naked flesh. What was wrong with her?

It wasn't her fault, she told herself. Cass had been needling her. She wasn't going to fall for that trick again. "You're reading far more into our relationship than is actually there, Mr. Cassidy," she alibied.

"I suggest we stop bandying words and get to the store."

Closing the front door and locking it behind them, Ms. Laurel Phillips, Dr. John Cassidy, and a large, happy-go-lucky, black Newfoundland stepped into the bright spring sun of the crisp, mountain morning.

"Okay, folks," Laurel said as her tiny staff gathered in the back room of the small market, "here's what's happened." The rest of her story was punctuated with assorted exclamations from Sandy and Dave. "Anyway," she concluded, "it's up to the four of us. I know Cass can't replace Frank as far as practical knowledge is concerned, but I thought an extra pair of hands might come in handy. Dave, do you know enough to take over the meat case?"

The young man nodded enthusiastically, obviously pleased for the chance to prove himself.

"Good. Consider yourself promoted," Laurel stated simply. "The rest of us will have to play it by ear. As a crisis arises, we'll just have to deal with it. Any questions?"

Sandy raised her hand. "Laurel, I hate to mention it, but I think today is the day the order goes in."

Sighing, Laurel agreed. "You're right. That's number one. You and Cass can put it together while I watch the registers."

"Me?" Sandy squeaked. "But I've never worked the computer recorder before."

"Well, neither have I, but how hard can it be?" Laurel asked.

"If you knew my reputation with machines, you

wouldn't ask," Sandy said with a pained expression. "The cash register just barely tolerates me since I accidentally poured a cup of cold coffee into it." Her brow wrinkled further. "Please?" Sandy begged. "I know I'll screw up the order and we'll get hundreds of cases of something we'll never sell."

"Okay, okay," Laurel conceded. She turned to the grinning Cass. "Do you think you can behave yourself long enough to tackle the order with me?"

"Sure," he said stoically. "We can't let a little machine buffalo us, or the word will get out and we'll be taken over by the coffee maker in cahoots with the chicken cooker."

"Very funny," Laurel said with trepidation. "Okay, troops, to your posts." She reached for the order book, light-sensitive pen, and recorder. "I don't know," she muttered, thumbing through the book, "this looks pretty confusing. I wonder how we go about it."

Cass relieved her of the spiral-bound book, turning to the first few pages. "I have an idea," he said dryly. "Let's read the instructions."

"The what? Let's see, smart aleck," she demanded, pulling the large book out of his hands. He was right, and of course he intended to rub it in. "Well, say it and get it over with," she said. "Tell me how much smarter you are, so we can get to work.

"I don't have to say a word," he smirked. "You just did it for me."

Laurel just shook her head, wishing she could wipe that sarcastic smile off his face.

Together, they walked up and down the aisles making notes in the order book, then retreated to the back room to record the order for transcription over the phone to the supplier. The whole operation went so smoothly, Laurel couldn't help wondering if they had done it correctly. It seemed too simple. She had taken charge, and Cass had followed her directions. Still, she'd feel better when the order was delivered and she could check its accuracy. Like Sandy, though she was reluctant to admit it, Laurel felt ill at ease with machines and computers.

"Whew," she sighed at last. "I'm glad that's over." Her feet were once again protesting the cramped quarters of her shoes, reminding her of her earlier decision to go shopping. "Hey, listen, Cass," she began, "I'm going to run down the street for a minute. Tell the others I'll be right back, will you?"

He shrugged, gathering up the ordering equipment and putting it away neatly. "Want some company for protection?"

"No thanks," she said. "It's broad daylight. I'm sure I'll be fine. I'm just going down to the dry goods store. Besides, you have work to do. The produce case needs restocking. If you need help, just ask Dave. Be back soon," she called, hurrying down the aisle and out the front door.

Choosing the light blue sneakers was easy. The jeans were something else altogether. "Are you sure they're supposed to fit like this?" Laurel questioned the salesgirl. "They seem awfully tight."

"That's the idea," the friendly girl assured her.

Laurel twisted in front of the mirror, looking over her shoulder at the denim material molding itself to her well-rounded figure. The pants did for her lower half what her sweater did for the upper portions of her anatomy, leaving no doubt that she was every inch a woman. "I don't know," Laurel mumbled to herself. "Maybe they're too tight to be decent." They were making her feel half embarrassed, half proud of what she saw.

Still turning in front of the mirror, she asked the salesgirl about possible shrinkage and was assured the jeans would remain just as they were. "They'd better," Laurel quipped, "or I'll have to be melted down and poured into them." Laughing, Laurel gathered up her city clothes, paid her bill, and bounced out of the store.

She felt good. Her feet no longer hurt, and judging from the heads she turned on her way back to the market, she obviously looked good, too. Nothing, however, prepared her for the reactions she got from her co-workers.

Sandy raised her eyebrows at her boss's new image, then congratulated her. "You look great," the girl said, genuinely impressed. "Now you're starting to look like a real country girl."

Blushing, Laurel went toward the back of the store to stow her old finery.

Cass saw her coming. His eyes ran appreciatively up and down the feminine curves encased in the tight denim. "Whew!" he said, cocking his head.

"Is it all right?" Laurel asked, concerned. "I was afraid maybe they were too small." At least he would tell her the truth, as he was so fond of doing.

"Are you asking my opinion?" Cass queried slowly.

"Well, yes," she said, "but don't be too blunt. I have a pretty tender ego."

He placed his hands gently on her shoulders, drawing her eyes to his deep, azure gaze. "Lady, you look beautiful," he said quietly. "My only problem now is going to be defending you against half the men in this town, never mind good old Frank."

"Meaning?"

"You're a very sexy lady in those jeans," he explained tenderly. "The new Laurel is blossoming into a surprise of natural beauty, just like the spring wild flowers on the hills around here." Watching the crimson creep to her cheeks, Cass smiled. "When you blush, you look like the wild rose of Sharon we saw on the way to work this morning. Very lovely."

She used her arms to push his hands off her shoulders. "Knock it off, Cassidy," she said crisply. "I'm not interested in that kind of comment. Am I decent or not?"

Sighing, Cass shook his head. "You're fine," he said. "The picture of propriety." Laurel was beginning to relax, until he finished his statement. "All you need is a staple in your navel, and you could pass for a centerfold in a men's magazine," he teased.

"Oh!" Laurel hissed loudly, "I can see I won't get a reasonable answer from you, so let's drop the subject." Whirling, she stuffed her old clothes into an empty carton and grabbed an apron, tying the strings tightly around her slim waist. How dare he! Did she really look sexy? No one had ever described her that way before, at least not to her knowledge. It was indecent. After all, she was a professional person, in spite of Cass's suggestions to the contrary, a woman with a certain image to protect. But that was in Ohio, she reminded herself. This was the wilds of California. Ooh, that man. He had no right. He . . . Laurel thought of Cass, her hazel eyes darkening to a translucent green as she sought him out and watched him work, trimming the vegetables and placing them in the cooler. She supposed he had complimented her, in his own way. He couldn't help it if his refinement didn't equal her own. Sexy. Humph! Not her. Not Laurel Phillips. She was above the scope of a description like that.

Before the day was over, however, she had decided to return to the dry goods store to purchase two more pairs of jeans in the same size as her first pair. After all, this was the country, and they certainly were the most comfortable and practical way to dress. Of course, Cass's comments had absolutely no bearing on her choice of wardrobe. She was merely fitting herself into her new environment, and she didn't care one whit whether her looks pleased him or not.

The most surprising thing was, Laurel believed her own rationalizations.

Chapter Five

Living with Cass was becoming easier, day by day, as he and Laurel shared the little house on the hill. Since that first kiss, he'd left her alone, but having him around had begun to be as natural as breathing to her, even if they did have their differences. When she stopped to think about it, Laurel wondered if losing him would not be a little like drowning. How could someone so unlike her become such an integral part of her life? She was used to being a loner, had always relished her solitary life-style—until now. In the space of one week, he'd succeeded in fitting himself into her life in such a way that she knew she'd never be the same again. Nor did she want to be.

Cass saw everything so differently. Small beauties that Laurel had always overlooked were seldom missed by his penetratingly clear observations of the world around them. He opened her eyes and her consciousness to a part of her existence she used to miss entirely. Perhaps his influence would remain with her. Remain. Laurel stiffened at the thought. She could no longer deny she would miss him when he left. He hadn't pressed her about finding someone else to stay with her. She'd heard through the grapevine that Frank had left town, but she kept forgetting to mention it to Cass.

Every time she started to think about her future, Laurel found a knot tightening in the pit of her stomach. Rationally, she wanted to be done with Julian and return to Ohio, but there was another, deeper, part of her that wished she could make time stand still. Her idea of heaven was rapidly becoming springtime in Julian, where life was simpler and filled with the gentle, wise man with the sandy-colored beard who had opened her horizons to the wonders of life and living.

Payday was admittedly a favorite time for Dave and Sandy. As Laurel prepared their weekly checks, she considered Cass. Since he was a part-timer, she knew she could give him cash. Slipping the bills into a plain envelope, she gathered up the checks for the other two and went to pay her staff.

It had been a long day, made far longer by the knowledge that seven whole days had passed. In less than three weeks, Rob and Joan would be home, and Laurel's fairy-tale existence would end.

Sandy and Dave received their checks gladly, bid her good night, and headed home. Cass was straightening up the back room. Standing unobserved in the doorway, Laurel watched him work. He'd been more than a good employee; he'd been a joy to have around. His upbeat attitudes were contagious.

Her mind reached out to touch him, her thoughts

caressing the smooth skin her senses wouldn't let her forget. Laurel felt the sensation of his beard on her face as if it had stroked her cheek only moments before. Why hadn't he shown any further interest in her? she wondered. Her tight jeans had caused an initial reaction, but nothing more. It wasn't as if she were throwing herself at him, she reasoned plausibly, but nothing she had done during the past week had seemed to faze him.

When they had first met, Cass had mentioned another woman. Perhaps his old love still stood in the way. Perhaps it always would.

Cass turned, a smile lighting his face when he spied her.

"Hi," Laurel said, her spirits dampened and her body frustrated by her earlier thoughts.

"Hi." He noticed her mood almost immediately. "Why so glum?"

"I guess I'm just tired," Laurel lied. "Here's your first week's pay. I'm sorry it couldn't be more. You've really earned your keep around here. I don't know what we would have done without you. Thanks."

"You're welcome," he answered as he took the envelope, folded it, and stuffed it in his pocket, "I have an idea," he began. "Since we're both tired, how about letting me take you out to dinner, now that I'm independently wealthy?" He patted the pocket containing his wages.

"No, no," Laurel protested, "I can't let you do that."

"You can't refuse," he argued. "You've been feeding Bear and me for a whole week. It's only fair that you let me return the favor. Unless, of course, you don't want to be seen dining with the hired help."

She started to defend herself against the slur, then stopped. She wasn't up to an argument. "Okay, Cassidy, but only if we go to the local café. I understand the food is excellent and inexpensive. You can't afford anything fancy on the wages I pay you."

"That's not my biggest problem," he chuckled. "Without a car, my choices are severely limited."

Laurel couldn't help smiling. "You're right," she said. "Without a fairy godmother, we're stuck in town. Personally, I'm glad. Let's close up and go eat."

Working together, they secured the store in the space of a few minutes, locked the front door, and walked up the narrow street. Bear trotted questioningly after them, giving the distinct impression he thought they were lost. The evening air still held a touch of winter's chill, despite the fact that spring had officially arrived.

When Laurel shivered, Cass slipped his arm nonchalantly around her shoulders, guiding her up the wooden steps and through the door of the quaint café. Bear was left outside to find himself a spot and wait.

When Cass touched her, Laurel savored the moment, wishing the café had been farther away so she could have relished his arm around her for a longer time. It wasn't as if he had kissed her. Still, the physical act of sheltering her was better than having him ignore the fact that she was a woman. This past week, he had treated her almost like a sister, and Laurel was very conscious of the fact that she didn't view Cass as her brother. Not at all.

The polished hardwood floor of the small restaurant reflected the antique oak furniture and filigreed frames around the portraits of Julian's founders and their families that lined the paneled walls. Only one table was available, near the front bay windows with lace curtains. Cass held a chair for Laurel, then slid into the one across from her. "We were lucky to get in," he observed. "This place is really crowded."

"Friday night," she reasoned. "Payday."

He nodded.

A friendly but harried waitress brought them menus, then disappeared into the crowd of small, square tables filled with diners.

"Prime rib sounds good," Cass said. "How about it?"

"But that's the most expensive thing on the menu!"

Smiling across the table, Cass raised one eyebrow. "So?"

"So, don't you want to save some of your pay for other things?"

"It won't take it all to feed you properly," he said, "Besides, you're worth it."

Laurel blushed, averting her eyes. "Okay, this is your party," she muttered. "Medium rare."

"To match the color of your cheeks," he teased. "Very appropriate."

How she managed to eat all her dinner, Laurel had no idea. Somehow, her thoughts kept wandering to the engagingly charming and unnerving man sitting across from her. She hardly tasted the food that went into her mouth.

"Dessert?" Cass asked when she had finished.

"Oh, no, thanks," she said slowly. "I'm stuffed, but go ahead, if you want. I understand they have delicious homemade apple pie here. This whole area is famous for its apples."

"I know." Cass peered out the window to the street below. "Poor Bear is still waiting for us," he observed. "Instead of dessert, let's get on home, give him his dinner, and relax by a roaring fire, okay?"

"Sounds great," Laurel replied. It really did. Curling up by the fire with Cass seemed to her to be one of the most pleasant aspects of her life right now. With each day, she found herself looking forward more and more to the peaceful evenings with him, talking, listening, or simply enjoying each other's presence. Being with Cass was, she admitted reluctantly, the best thing that had ever happened to her.

No one at the store had raised an eyebrow when he had continued to show up for work. They simply accepted him as an equal and a friend. Laurel envied the natural way he seemed to fit in wherever he went.

Cass paid the check, left a substantial tip, and helped Laurel with her coat before guiding her out the door with a hand placed gently at her elbow.

There was that touch again. She held her breath, hoping it would continue, but he released her when they reached the street.

Both of them were silent as they headed for home, Bear walking contentedly beside Laurel.

Without really thinking about it, Cass grasped Laurel's hand in his, then pulled away. "I'm sorry," he said quietly, "that was a slip."

She looked up at him affectionately. "Don't be sorry. I liked it." Placing her hand back in his, she gave it a little squeeze. "Besides, it's warmer this way," she reasoned, grasping him tightly until he relaxed and returned the gesture. Hand in hand, they turned the corner and began the climb to the house.

Oh, lady, Cass thought silently as they walked, if you only knew what you're beginning to do to me. I was all right till now, but touching you again was a mistake. You're so vulnerable, in spite of your education and degrees. Inside that professional exterior you project is a little girl who needs me, damn it, and I don't want to love you. Elizabeth was enough. She should have cured me for good, but you—you with all your innocence and beauty—you've gotten under my skin.

"A penny for your thoughts," Laurel remarked lightheartedly.

Unconsciously, he squeezed her hand, then released it. "Not for a hundred dollars," he said seriously, "Not on your life."

Sobered by his unusual tone, Laurel slid her cold hands into the pockets of her jacket, remaining quiet the rest of the way home. I shouldn't have insisted on holding his hand, she decided. He obviously doesn't feel attracted to me, physically or emotionally, and I embarrassed him. She felt the sting of unshed tears pooling in her eyes. He's right, she told herself, we should mean nothing to each other. Why that thought caused her such pain, Laurel had no idea, unless . . . No. She couldn't, she mustn't, fall for Cass. He's a drifter, a ne'er-do-well who may leave any day. To allow herself to care for him would be asking for disaster. She must control her emotions as she always had in the past. Rationally, that seemed to be the answer to her dilemma. Unfortunately, Laurel's emotions cried out with bitter honesty that it was already too late to regain her heart.

Taking Laurel's key, Cass unlocked the door, switched on the light, and began piling kindling and logs in the fireplace. Bear sought out his dish of dry dog food and Laurel went to hang her coat in her room.

Contemplating her future without Cass, Laurel felt a catch in her throat. The sensation strangely resembled panic, and she realized just how lonely her life had been before meeting him.

Hurrying back to the living room, she rounded the corner and ran full force into Cass's broad, warm chest. His arms went out automatically to steady her. Then, as if having a mind of their own, they pulled her tightly to him, pinning her against his hard-muscled body.

"Damn," he murmured resignedly.

Laurel tilted her face up to his, caressing him with the liquid gold of her eyes.

He was through fighting. His lips descended tenderly to claim hers and the unexpected fire they found there ignited a tempest within him. Moving over her face, Cass's mouth gently investigated her cheeks and closed eyes, then returned to her moist, slightly parted lips.

This was what she had waited for, hoped for, all evening. Almost beyond control, Laurel languished in the feel of his kisses, his masculine body, and his thigh angling firmly between her legs. Dear Lord! She'd never wanted anyone like this before, even in her wildest dreams. Something inside her jarred Laurel back to the reality of the present. If she didn't stop herself now, there would be no chance. "Please—Cass—please," she begged.

"Laurel," he moaned, covering her with feathery kisses made even more tantalizing by the touch of his beard across her sensitive skin.

"No, Cass," Laurel pleaded, unconvincingly.

"Why?" he asked raggedly. "Your body is telling me yes."

She pushed herself to arm's length, breathless from their contact. A deep, probing ache knotted her stomach, but she persisted, "We hardly know each other."

Releasing her, Cass strode to the hearth, stirring the fire with the poker. "How long is your usual date, Laurel?" he asked. "How many hours do you spend with each man, each time?"

What did that have to do with anything? "Why?" she asked aloud.

"Think about it," he continued. "You and I have been together constantly for, let's see . . . over two hundred hours straight. At four hours per date, we would have had more than fifty. I've known you the

WINTER'S PROMISE

equivalent of a whole year, Laurel, and that's definitely long enough to be allowed to kiss you."

"Maybe," she said, "but was that all you wanted?"

"You know the answer to that," he concluded dryly. "Any woman would. You wanted me, too, and you know it."

"No."

"I'm not going to argue about something as important as loving, Laurel. Search your heart, be honest with yourself, then tell me the truth."

"I *am* telling you the truth," she insisted vehemently.

"No, Laurel. You can't be truthful about wanting to be with me unless you see the truth inside yourself first. I don't think you've done that yet." Solemnly, Cass seated himself at one end of the couch, facing the fire, and propped his booted feet on the raised hearth.

Truth? How could she tell him the truth—that she cared deeply for him, that she ached when she looked at him, that he had enriched her life, and that thoughts of his leaving tore her apart. His body beckoned to hers every waking moment, and she yearned for that intense closeness her imagination could hardly fathom. To confess her real feelings would be foolish as well as dangerous. Cass wouldn't understand. If there was one thing Laurel had learned since childhood, it was never to let her guard down with anyone. His anger was proof enough that she was right.

Her heart still pounded, partly from his kisses and partly as a reaction to his rapid change in mood when she had stopped him from loving her. No, she corrected, not loving but making love—two very different things. It would be foolishly naive to allow herself to think that he loved her as much as she loved him.

Laurel's breath caught in her throat as her mind repeated the impossible revelation. She loved him! Now what? She sighed inwardly, closing her eyes. What had happened to all her impenetrable defenses? Laurel smiled, slowly accepting the idea. Cass happened, that's what, she mused. Happiness filled her. Cass.

But he was angry. She had to convince him to forgive her so they could restore their former rapport. He didn't need to be told she loved him. That was her secret.

Each evening, they had relaxed by the fire with a bowl of popcorn. Perhaps a repetition of the familiar scene would take the chill out of the atmosphere in the tiny house. Laurel decided it was worth a try and the odor of the freshly popped corn shortly filled the tiny rooms.

With the warm bowl in one hand, Laurel paused behind the couch, looking down lovingly at the soft brown of Cass's hair. She placed one hand on his shoulder, barely able to keep the touch from turning into a caress.

He tilted his head back against the cushions, gazing up at her.

"Popcorn?" she asked, popping a fresh kernel into his unprotesting mouth.

Patting the cushion next to him, Cass motioned for Laurel to join him.

She kicked off her shoes and gladly seated herself in the spot he'd indicated. Taking another kernel in her fingers, she fed it to him, her touch lingering on his lips. How do we go back, she wondered, back to each other's embrace, where we both want to be?

Laurel returned her hand to the bowl, selected one kernel for herself, placed it slowly in her mouth while Cass watched, and sensuously licked the butter off her fingertips.

"Laurel," he groaned, "don't tease if you don't intend to do anything about it."

He looked so depressed, so desirable, and so dear, that just watching his struggle for control made her heart twist for him. The time would come for him to leave, that much was inevitable, and what would she have then? They could never arrange their futures so they could be together; all they had was the present. And here we sit wasting it, she thought, both of us miserable, even if it is for different reasons. The question was, could she give without expecting an equal return? Her answer came as an unbelievable yearning to belong to him, no matter what.

She placed the bowl on the coffee table. "Cass," she whispered, with the double meaning tearing her apart, "love me."

His hand cupped her cheek tenderly, drawing her face closer to his own. "I won't press you," he said, "I'll leave now if you want."

With one hand resting lightly on his thigh, the other finding its way around his neck, Laurel wanted to tell him to stay forever, that her love would find a way, but she knew those words were a lie. "No," she finally said, quietly. "Stay and be with me."

His expression took on an aura of revealing sensitivity coupled with growing passion. For a moment, his eyes continued to search her face, then, satisfied that she meant to be his, he enveloped her in his feverish embrace. "Laurel," he whispered, "you won't be sorry. I promise."

No. She wouldn't be sorry, of that she was sure. As her arms found their way around him, she held him with an intensity born of desperation, clutching at him as if to ward off the inevitability of their eventual parting. Soon, he would be lost to her, but until then . . . "Oh, Cass," she breathed softly, "let's not waste any more time."

Kissing her tenderly, Cass rose from the couch and drew her up with him. "When you make up your mind, you're a very determined lady, aren't you?" he asked softly. "Come here."

Laurel placed her palms on his chest, reveling in the taut feel of him, remembering how irresistably tempting he had felt when she had brushed off the hair from his back.

"This time, you can touch as much as you want," he said, also recalling the way she had affected him with her errant caresses.

Blushing, Laurel focused her eyes on the fine, soft hairs of his chest as she unbuttoned his shirt and slipped her hands inside the smooth fabric to explore his warm, masculine body. She tilted back her head, welcoming his probing kiss with an incredible yearning that throbbed through her in an explosion of sweeping desire.

His lips crushed hers, then moved over them in an

erotic blending of motion and rising passion that joined them in an ecstasy of shared feeling. Pulling her against his hard warmth, Cass's hands found their way beneath her sweater, traveling over her back in sweet torment.

She wanted him to touch her, to caress her, to blot out reality, until nothing else mattered. Reaching back with one hand, she grasped his forearm, guiding his hand forward to cup her firm breast.

Moaning audibly, Cass buried his face in the hollow of her shoulder, gently fondling the treasure she led him to, then reclaimed her soft, invitingly parted lips while he lifted her sweater.

Laurel heard, then felt, his reaction to her near-nakedness. His breath was ragged, his mouth insistent, as he sought the bud of her breast through the thin ivory lace of her bra. With her eyes closed, she unhooked the offending garment and discarded it.

The dying fire gave her skin a golden, flickering glow. Laurel was more graceful, more appealing, than any woman Cass had ever imagined. He was almost afraid to move for fear of breaking the spell of her erotic beauty. "My God, Laurel," he whispered hoarsely, "I never dreamed . . ."

Placing her fingers over his lips, Laurel hushed him. Just hearing his voice, remembering how little time they had left, was edging her closer and closer to tears. She musn't spoil it for him, she thought. If she could immerse herself in the physical side of love and ignore the emotional, she'd be fine. He would never guess the truth.

Cass kissed her soft fingertips on his lips, moving

down to place another kiss in her palm before removing his shirt. Barechested, he pulled the unprotesting Laurel against his gleaming body with the tender roughness of unfulfilled desire. His powerful hands stroked her bare flesh, finally sliding into the waist of her jeans and finding the snap. Gentle fingers eased the tight denim and lace over her hips and down, intimately tracing the curves of her delicately rounded figure.

She stepped out of her clothes to stand before him, unashamed.

Cass's face was a study in tender awe as his liquid blue gaze melted any reserves she had left. Taking her hand, he led her away from the fireplace and the heat of the burning logs.

Questioningly, Laurel looked into his sensitive expression.

"My bed," he said quietly, opening his sleeping bag and spreading it out on the floor. "The lady comes to my bed, such as it is."

"I don't mind," Laurel assured him, "as long as you're there, too." She lowered herself onto the flannel lining and watched with growing excitement as Cass quickly removed his boots, then stripped off the rest of his clothes.

She couldn't take her eyes off him. Oh, Lord, how she loved him. What had begun as a simple physical attraction had blossomed into much, much more.

Cass lowered himself into her outstretched arms, their first touch loosing a surge of delirious passion. They fell into each other's embrace, trembling with the thrill of discovery and escalating sensuality,

WINTER'S PROMISE

their damp, heated kisses feeding the flames of yearning.

Every nerve in Laurel's body tingled, becoming almost too much to bear when Cass's beard followed a teasing trail of kisses down her neck and over her soft flesh, pausing to tantalize her breasts before descending even lower. It was marvelous, but not enough. There was only one way she could get enough of Cass.

Laurel moaned and slid her body along the length of his. Easing him over her, she gladly welcomed his thrusting hardness to the dark warmth of her own need.

Her name escaped his lips as he claimed her, seeming to come from the depths of his soul and binding them in a timeless, endless belonging.

Savoring the intensity of the moment, Laurel was lost in the heated frenzy of his lovemaking, enveloped by his strength, his possessive lust, his surging rhythm, and his ultimate gentleness. How could he hold back? She wanted him so much she could hardly contain herself. She wanted to scream and plead for him to love her. Finally, it was more than she could bear. "Cass," she moaned, "please, please, now!"

With a cry, they joined in the ultimate possession, no longer able to resist fulfillment.

His intensity consumed her completely and her senses erupted in a wild mixture of intense pleasure and bewildering pain. She gasped at the unique intimacy, the unbelievable joy, he had given her.

Breathing heavily, Cass levered himself over her. "Are you all right?" he asked with deep concern.

"I'm sorry. I meant to be more gentle, but—my God, Laurel—you're so very beautiful."

Laurel looked at him with tears brimming in her eyes, thankful for the cover of darkness in the dimly-lit room. He was concerned about her body, the part of her that had answered his hard-muscled flesh with unbridled abandon. No, her body was fine, better than ever, she admitted ruefully. It was the other side of her that was hurting beyond belief. She loved a man who could never be hers, with every fiber of her being. "I—I'm okay," she choked, but it was no use. Tears began spilling out of the corners of her eyes, running down her temples and into her tousled, love-mussed hair.

Cass's thumb brushed her cheek, seeking the wetness he sensed was there. "You're crying. I hurt you, didn't I?" The agony he felt was reflected in his voice.

"No, really," she sobbed. "I—I'm just . . ."

Folding her in his arms, Cass covered them both with one side of the sleeping bag. "Here," he joked, trying to lift her spirits, "I'll hug you and make it all better, just like when you were a little girl."

Laurel felt like an absolute fool, but she couldn't stop crying. "No—nobody did," she cried. "Nobody ever hugged me."

"Oh, come on, Laurel," he urged, "surely, somebody did. What about your parents?"

"No," she said flatly, sniffling. "Only my grandmother had the time for things like that."

"See? I told you so."

WINTER'S PROMISE

"But, but, you don't see," Laurel stammered. "When I was seven, she died." The sobbing began anew as the memories of her new love joined with the pain of her childhood.

"You mean, nobody has comforted you like this since then?" He was amazed.

She shook her head, burying her face against his arm and chest, secure, yet afraid of having already shown him too much of her tender, vulnerable, emotional self.

Cass pulled her closer, drying her tears with the corner of the sleeping bag. "Tell you what," he said. "We'll raise our kids with extra hugs to make up for it. In the meantime, I'll hug you twice as much, every time the mood strikes me. How's that?"

"Wh—what?" Laurel could hardly believe her ears. Children? The man was crazy, or, worse yet, patronizing. Did he think she was a complete fool? Children, indeed. He was going to leave her, just like her grandmother and her brother had, without warning. She'd allowed herself to lose her anchors when she was a child, when she knew no better. But this was different. No one else was going to get the chance to hurt her. She had been an idiot to get this involved with Cass. Well, the past was past, she thought, but she could prevent further commitments, even if she had to lie to him to do it. After all, he was lying to her with talk of children.

Laurel squirmed out of his arms, climbed to her feet, and faced him. "No, Cassidy," she exclaimed hotly. "Just plain no. No relationship between us, no future plans, no children. This was a fling, do you understand? It meant nothing to me. You must think I'm a real fool to try a line like *that* on me," she snapped defensively. "Why bother, anyway? You got what you wanted, didn't you?"

Turning, she left him lying on the floor, alone.

Cass looked after her as she slammed her bedroom door. "It was no line, Laurel," he said quietly to the empty room. "God help me, I wish it were."

Chapter Six

It was a long, long night for Laurel. Waking cold and miserable, she rolled herself up in the blankets that her tossing had pulled loose from the foot of the bed. Sighing, she closed her eyes against the bitter taste of morning. He was out there, with his tenderness and gentle, loving ways, and all she had done was cause them both misery. Ashamed, Laurel wanted nothing more than to retreat back into sleep.

The knock on her door was forceful and loud.

Refusing to answer, she ducked her head under her blankets.

"Laurel," Cass called, "you'd better be decent or you're going to blush again, because I'm coming in."

"No!"

"Yes," he contradicted, opening the door and letting Bear out. "You haven't eaten a decent breakfast for a week."

"I don't eat breakfast," she echoed.

"You do now," Cass told her firmly. He had come into the room carrying a tray and there was little doubt in Laurel's mind what was on it. She could smell the odors of bacon and eggs through the blankets. Ick!

"I hate food in the morning," Laurel screeched. "Go away."

Cass placed the tray on the night table. She felt the mattress sag to one side as he sat next to her. "Come on, sleepy head," he coaxed, "rise and shine."

"No," came the muffled reply. She couldn't look at him, not after last night. He should be furious with her, not bringing her breakfast. What kind of man was he, anyway? Laurel saw his fingers as they curled around the top of her covers and pried one corner away from her face.

"Hello, in there," he said, smiling.

"Hello," she whispered.

"Are you okay?" he asked with concern.

Laurel knew what he meant. How was she, after. . . ? As she looked up at him, her heart melted. Oh, how she loved him, in spite of her resolve not to. It was all she could do to keep from winding her arms around his neck and pulling him down to her. Grabbing the edges of her blankets out of his hands, she covered her face once again. "I'm fine," she insisted, "but I'm *not* hungry!"

"Oh yes you are," Cass cajoled. "Now, come on out and eat, or I'm coming in there."

"You wouldn't dare."

"You should know me better than that," he drawled.

He wouldn't. Laurel knew she was safe beneath the bedclothes. All she had to do was keep still and he'd eventually give up and leave her alone. Then she could crawl out of bed, make her way to the shower, and wake up slowly the way she always did. There was that hand again, intruding into her sanctuary. "No, Cass."

"Yes, Laurel," he said purposefully, giving her covers a swift jerk and sending them flying across the room to land in a jumbled heap on the floor.

"No!" Laurel gasped, as he exposed her to the cool morning air and his penetrating stare. She squirmed around, adjusting her long cotton gown to cover as much as she could.

With his hands on his hips, Cass was standing over her, smiling. "Now, sunshine, let's eat our breakfast," he reiterated.

Laurel pressed her lips tightly together, crossing her arms across her chest in defiance. "No," she mumbled.

His white teeth gleamed amidst the neatly trimmed whiskers. Reaching for the fork on the tray, Cass speared a piece of egg and sat back down. "Open up," he ordered.

She shook her head violently, closing her eyes.

Strong fingers pinched her nostrils. He was serious! Laurel opened her mouth to protest and found it filled with the forkful of egg. It would be crass to spit it out, even if he *did* deserve to be decorated with it. She had to chew and swallow it. Edging away from him, Laurel sat up and finished the mouthful.

"Good girl," he praised, ignoring the angry flashing of her eyes.

When he came at her again, she was ready. No more passive resistance for Laurel. This time, she'd give him a taste of his own medicine. Grabbing the arm that held the fork, she threw all her weight against his advancing bulk.

"Oh, so you want to play rough?" he grinned. "Well, that's fine with me."

The fork remained almost stationary, in spite of Laurel's efforts, while Cass's other hand encompassed first one of her wrists then the other. She was losing the physical end of the confrontation. Now, it was up to her wits to get her out of this. "Cass," she exclaimed breathlessly, "be sensible!" He had her in a helpless position, her hands together in front of her, and by some miracle of balance he still had the forkful of egg.

"I am being sensible, Laurel," he said. "You should eat breakfast."

"I'm sure you're right," she agreed lamely, forcing her tense shoulders to relax appreciably, "but this is a most awkward position. Couldn't you let go a little?"

Every muscle in his body was tightly drawn. She could see the tensed strength beneath his clothes.

The knee that was pressed so intimately against her thigh withdrew slightly. "And then what will you do?" he asked pointedly.

"We can discuss it like two normal adults," she answered, a bit too truthfully.

"Nope," Cass countered, pulling her wrists closer to his chest. "Knowing you, that means you've already made up your mind."

She had to stall for time to think. "Why don't you eat it? You're the one that's so gung ho for breakfast."

"Good idea," he said, grinning at her. "Wrestling

always makes me hungry." Settling back onto the edge of the bed, he put the egg into his mouth, returned the fork to the tray, and picked up a strip of crisp bacon in his free hand.

He had relaxed his hold ever so slightly, and Laurel feigned a casual pose, resting on her haunches, waiting for the right moment.

Cass bit off the end of the strip of bacon. "You know, Laurel," he said when he had eaten it, "I was only trying to do something nice, to break the ice between us this morning. I wasn't sure just how mad you might be, and I racked my brain for some way to approach you."

This was an unusual approach, she thought, but he wasn't fooling her. All he wanted was . . . The thought of his lovemaking affected her almost as if it were happening right then. Her pulse sped, her face flushed, her eyes widened, and her abdomen knotted with an unbelievable yearning for him. She had to stay calm, convince him everything was fine, and then run. If she could lock herself in the bathroom, he'd have time to cool off and realize she wasn't going to succumb to his masculine charms again. She could not, for her own sake.

"You know," she said, "that bacon almost smells good. Why don't you release me so I can try some?"

"Why don't I just feed you?" he grinned.

"Don't you think that's rather childish? I resent being treated like that."

His smiling face took on a more somber tone. "You're right. I'm sorry," he apologized, setting her free. "I was afraid you wouldn't talk to me at all, and I think we need to discuss some things."

"Of course," she said, hardly hearing him. Her mind was churning, trying to choose the precise moment to flee. His head turned momentarily toward the breakfast tray, and Laurel jumped from the bed, but the long skirt of her nightgown slowed her as it whipped around her legs. The door was within reach when a strong hand tightened around her arm. The momentum from her headlong flight carried her in a semicircle. Breathless and angry, she crashed into Cass's immovable body. "Damn you," she hissed. "Let me go."

Holding her close, he spoke softly. "You don't have to run from me, Laurel. I'll never keep you against your will."

"Like on the bed?"

"I was playing with you, and I thought you saw it as a game, too," he said solemnly.

"A game?" she sputtered.

"Yes, my love, a game, the kind two grown people play from time to time, just to have fun with each other. All you had to do to get away was to tell me you weren't amused."

Amused? Hardly. The man was impossible. He'd made her feel trapped and angry for the sake of sport. Ah, but if she had seen it as the game he had said it was, it wouldn't have affected her that way, would it? From the sad look on his face, she couldn't help believing him. A game. Laurel shook her head and sighed as her hands found their way around his waist to rest lightly on his ribs. "I don't understand you at all, Cassidy."

His arms lay loosely, encompassing her, and he looked lovingly into her face. You'd better go now," he whispered. "Breakfast is over."

Laurel's body was yearning to press tightly against his remembered sweetness. It was useless to try to fight it. She wanted him more desperately this morning than she had the night before, and he was telling her to go away, to leave him. That was the last thing she wanted to do. Cass had said to tell him if she wanted to be left alone. Perhaps if she indicated otherwise . . .

"Don't you think we should finish our breakfast?" she said lightly. "After all, we don't want to waste the food." Taking his hand, Laurel led the way back to her bed.

"No, Laurel, I don't think so," he said flatly.

"Oh, come on," she wheedled. "It's my turn, and you're spoiling the game." Reaching the tray, she speared a bit of the now cold egg. "Here," she smiled, "open up," and popped the bite into his mouth, her eyes begging him to come to her, her breasts rising and falling rapidly under the thin material of her gown.

"Laurel," he said roughly, "you know it isn't bacon and eggs I want, don't you?"

"Yes," she whispered, "I know."

"And you?" he asked slowly, hesitantly, as if he feared her answer.

"I think," she said very quietly, wrapping her arms around his neck, "that having you for breakfast may start a new trend in my life."

"You've already started something new in mine," he confided. "I can't leave you alone, and I know that's not fair to you."

Laurel smiled up at him. "You let me decide that, will you?"

"We both have some decisions to make, love," he reflected.

The game was beginning to get far too serious for Laurel's taste. He kept referring to decisions and their future, when there was no use. Reaching to the tray, she picked up a piece of cold bacon, backed toward the bed, and climbed up on the coverlet. "Come and get it," she teased, moving swiftly out of his reach.

"So, you want to play, do you?" he grinned, lunging for her and pinning her to the mattress. "I have a marvelous game in mind."

"I'll bet you do," she said huskily, as he lowered himself to her.

This time, she wouldn't try to run from him. There would be no recriminations, no old memories to keep them apart, nothing to spoil their closeness. All that mattered was this moment, to be in his arms and belong to him in a way that only lovers understood.

Laurel closed her eyes, imagining not only Cass's lovemaking, but his love. Pretending she had his love in return for hers would make the moment even sweeter. She smiled.

"You have the happiest look I've ever seen," he said, kissing her forehead. "What are you thinking?"

"About you," she said, "and how marvelous it feels to be in your arms, to have you love me."

WINTER'S PROMISE

"Believe me, Laurel," he whispered, "it's my pleasure. Now, how about taking your nightgown off so I can look at you?"

Laurel wiggled out of her gown while Cass removed his clothes, his gaze never leaving her. She blushed under the persistant stare.

"What do you know," he said, "when you blush, you do it all over!"

Grabbing the pillow, Laurel swung it at him.

Cass ducked, wresting it from her and covering her nakedness with his own.

They both laughed, then grew suddenly silent in the tenderness of the moment.

Wide-eyed, Laurel looked into his beloved face, her lips trembling with desire as he proceeded to join them once more, gently and unselfishly.

Time had vanished in a velvet mist of ebbing and flowing emotion. Laurel snuggled closer to Cass, reveling in the afterglow of his lovemaking. "Mmm," she sighed, "you're improving with practice."

"Thanks, I think." He planted a kiss on the top of her head which was nestled in the crook of his arm. Cass gave her a little squeeze. "I hate to mention it, but don't you think we should be getting to work? We can change the bedding later and get rid of the bacon crumbs." He was chuckling.

"The crumbs were your fault," she mumbled. "This was your game."

"But you play it so well."

"Thank you." She wrapped one arm over his chest,

and scooted up to kiss first his cheek, then his lips. "What time is it?"

He told her.

"Oh," she said languidly. Then, realizing what he had said, she squeaked, "Oh, no!"

Cass was laughing. "We're going to be late, Ms. Phillips."

"But we have to open! No one can get in until we do."

"In that case," he grinned, "may I suggest we save time and share the bathroom?"

Laurel blushed. It was rather ludicrous; she had just spent over an hour making love to the man. Under the circumstances, false modesty was unnecessary, and time was of the essence. "Oh, I don't care, just get moving!" she shouted as she ran to the dresser, digging through her blouses for something to wear. Thank goodness her jeans were ready. Now, all they had to do was stop time and get down the hill to the market in less than two minutes.

Cass had the shower turned on and the temperature adjusted by the time she had grabbed two towels and joined him.

Watching the rivulets of water trace her curves, he found his thoughts wandering. "I wish we had more time," he told her, touching her gently, his hands following the path of the droplets.

"Well, we don't," Laurel said, slapping his wet buttocks playfully, "so don't get any more ideas."

"Me?" he protested. "Who started the game over again?"

Laurel jumped out and quickly toweled herself

dry. "Knock off the talk, Cassidy," she ordered fondly, "we're already five minutes late."

"Yes, ma'am," he quipped. "Your hair is all wet."

"So's yours," she retorted.

Cass stood on the porch tucking in his shirttails while Laurel closed and locked the house. "I thought men got dressed faster than women," she prompted. "Come on. Hurry."

"Hiking boots take longer to lace than tennis shoes," he countered. "Besides, you have more incentive than I do. You're the boss."

"Don't remind me," she grumbled. "I take my jobs seriously. This is unforgivable."

"But understandable," he grinned, grasping her hand. "Come on. I'll race you."

"I don't run," she insisted. "At least, not usually."

"I'll wager you've done a lot of things lately that you don't usually do," he teased, "For instance—"

"Shut up, Cassidy," she interrupted, starting off at a slow trot, "and run."

Hand in hand they descended the steep incline with a speed that truly amazed her, reaching the bottom in what seemed like mere seconds.

The situation was worse than Laurel had imagined. Not only were Sandy and Dave waiting, but several customers as well.

Reaching the corner at a dead run, Laurel was overtaken by her momentum, slightly turning her ankle. Without hesitation, Cass scooped her up in his arms, carrying her the last few yards to the door.

"General delivery," he joked. "Did one of you order a boss lady?"

Sandy giggled when Laurel insisted loudly, "Put me down."

Setting her on her feet, Cass stepped back while Laurel unlocked the door turning to the customers apologetically. "I'm sorry. Please be patient. We'll open in a few minutes."

Laurel let the staff in and relocked the door. "Okay," she said, "let's see how fast we can get this place ready for business."

All Dave did was raise his eyebrows, grin sheepishly at Cass, and head for the butcher counter. Sandy was still giggling.

"Oh, for goodness sake, Sandy," Laurel snapped, "what's so funny?"

"I'm sorry, Laurel, I really am. It's just that you both look like you were caught in a monsoon without an umbrella."

"It's the hair, Laurel," Cass explained. "I told you we should have taken more time to dry off after our shower."

"Cass!" Laurel was mortified. How dare he allude to their personal relationship like that?

Cass turned to Sandy and caught Dave's eye one aisle away. "Listen, you two. I know what you're thinking, but it's all right, really." Cass reached past Laurel and picked up a fresh bunch of broccoli from the produce case, according it the tender care one would give a fresh posy of delicate flowers. Taking Laurel's hand in his, he dropped to one knee, clutching the broccoli bouquet to his heart.

"I realize this is sudden," Cass said with a straight face, "but will you do me the honor of becoming my wife?" A broad smile lit his countenance. "You needn't answer now. Just remember, I have witnesses."

Her mouth fell open. The man was crazy—honestly crazy. Laurel was left speechless.

"You see, Sandy," Cass gibed, getting to his feet, "the little lady is struck dumb by my offer to make an honest woman of her." He handed the broccoli bouquet to the cashier. "Perhaps you'd better put these in water for her. She seems a little overwhelmed at the moment. Now, let's get this store open," he ordered. "Snap to it!"

Laurel didn't believe what had just happened. She had had proposals of marriage before, but never one like that! Extraordinary. She felt as if Errol Flynn had swung down from the nearest parapet and swept her off her feet, complete with swashbuckling sword and plumed hat.

Cass disappeared into the back room, taking Laurel's illusion with him. Her eyes met Sandy's and both women burst into laughter.

"Can you believe it?" Sandy gasped, holding up the broccoli.

"That's what I call a practical suitor," Laurel laughed nervously. "I can eat his bouquet if I don't want to press it in my diary."

"You don't suppose he meant it do you?" the younger woman asked.

"No," Laurel answered quietly. "I don't suppose he did." Mechanically, she went about her morning tasks. In her imagination, Cass still knelt at her feet. They were in a castle, and Laurel was the gossamer-gowned princess, held prisoner by her duty to her subjects and her kingdom. Cass was the dashing hero sent to free her. It's too bad this isn't one of those sappy old movies, she mused. They always have happy endings.

Instead of returning the deep green bouquet to the produce case, Sandy had found an old, brown, coffee mug, filled it with water, and placed the whole arrangement on the desk in the store's office. Laurel had reached for it several times during the day, intending to dispose of the unsettling reminder of Cass's proposal, but something had always stayed her hand. As the day progressed, she began to see his teasing proposal as a cruelty. He was taunting her, offering something he knew he couldn't deliver. A joke was one thing, but that! She'd make it clear, as soon as they were alone, that she saw no humor in the situation. None at all.

Walking home, Laurel tried several times to broach the subject, but Cass kept avoiding the seriousness she sought. Finally, after dinner, he allowed her to instigate a real discussion of their relationship.

"I think your proposal today was in poor taste," Laurel began.

"Why?"

"Because marriage is no joke," she retorted.

"I know," he said quietly.

"If you know, why did you make it so silly?" she asked dryly.

"Suppose I'd approached you seriously, like the other night?" he asked. "Would you have listened, or would you have run from me again?"

"Cassidy, that's a hypothetical question with no bearing on this discussion."

"Is it?"

"It is, unless you really meant what you said, and I know that can't be."

"Why not?"

"Because we come from totally different worlds. Do you expect me to give up everything and go traipsing around the country living out of a sack?" she snapped.

"Would you?"

"Of course not," she insisted forcefully. "I have a career and sensible goals, even if you don't."

"But what about love, Laurel?"

"What about it? Are you suggesting I may be in love with you?"

"I would hope so, since you've seen fit to sleep with me," he said wryly.

"That has nothing to do with it," Laurel insisted, "I simply find you attractive. That's all." The whole situation was complicated enough without admitting to Cass that she loved him. He might do something even more rash if she told him the truth. No. It was best left the way it was. He obviously didn't understand her dedication to her career. How could he? And he'd be miserable trying to conform to her ideals.

Cass's probing eyes searched her hard mask of indifference sadly. "In that case, I guess I lose, Laurel. Because I love you. More than I had dreamed possible."

She couldn't face him. A declaration of love was the last thing she had expected and she could feel it destroying the wall of protection she had erected around her true feelings. "Cass, don't," she pleaded raggedly.

He came to stand behind her, his hands resting gently on her shoulders. "If you mean don't love you, that's impossible," he said. "I know. I've been fighting it, and it's no use. Like it or not, Laurel, I do love you."

"Will you stop saying that!"

"No. One of us has to say what we both feel."

"No," she said, clenching her teeth. "No." To admit her aching love was wrong, for both of them. If she did, Cass would continue to press her to marry him, and that was totally out of their reach. Did he expect her to give up all she had worked for, all she had planned? That was what he seemed to want. She'd never had a serious affair before, and if this was how it hurt she never intended to have another. There was a lot to be said for a solitary existence. It might be less exciting, but it certainly beat the heartwrenching pain she was feeling now. "Cass, I . . ."

He turned her in his arms and tilted her chin up with two fingers, kissing her gently. "Give it a little more time," he whispered. "It's a big step and you haven't been thinking about it as long as I have."

Oh how wrong you are, she thought. I've been thinking about little else for days. Still, she was no closer to an answer that would mend the tearing of her life. They had simply met, loved, and would soon part. There was nothing to decide. The futility of their situation overcame her and, throwing her

WINTER'S PROMISE

arms around his neck, Laurel reached her trembling lips to his. At his heated response, tears silently rolled down her cheeks, and she almost thought she saw a trace of moisture pooling in his misty, yearning gaze.

"Oh, Cass," she sobbed. "Hold me. Stay with me."

Lifting her easily, he carried her to the couch, laid her down, and sat beside her. "Don't cry, love," he said, drying her eyes. "Don't you know you're supposed to be happy when a man says he loves you?"

"I—I am happy," she said haltingly.

"Wow. I'd hate to see you sad," he teased gently. "We can work it out, Laurel, but you'll have to trust me." Cass drew the backs of his fingers over her smooth cheek, "Trust me."

"I—I've already trusted you with all of me," she stammered. Pulling him down to her, she wrapped her arms around him, entwining her fingers in his hair. Tomorrow would take care of itself. Tonight was all that mattered now. That, and being with Cass again.

"Oh, my love. So many decisions to make."

"Just one, at the moment," she whispered, letting her hands brush across his body.

Tensing, Cass pushed himself away. "No," he groaned. "If there's no future for us, Laurel, then there's no use making it worse."

Worse? Was he telling her that the perfect, beautiful, physical relationship between them was bad? "I—I don't understand," she whispered. "You said you loved me."

Cass stood and walked to the hearth. "I did and I do," he said. "That's why I can't make love to you again." He stuffed both hands in his pockets, his shoulders stooped with the weight of his decision.

"But I thought you wanted me," she said, her voice beginning to break.

He spun around. "Want you? My God, Laurel, you're tearing me apart! Of course, I want you, but I love you, too, and that makes the difference."

"I still don't understand," she said quietly, swinging her feet to the floor and sitting in a dejected huddle on the couch.

"If I didn't care—if it were a fling—it would be easy," Cass explained. "But you're special now, and it's not the same."

Laurel spoke almost inaudibly. "And before?"

"The first time," he said, facing her, "it was just a man and a woman, until something happened to me. I can't explain it."

"And the second time?" she whispered, awed.

He shrugged. "The second time, I tried to leave. I hadn't consciously intended to make love to you, only to apologize for the night before. Then, when you started to tease me, I wasn't prepared to resist. I lost control." More quietly, "I suppose I wanted to."

Laurel had come closer to him. "And now?"

"Now I've told you where we stand," he stated. "Go to bed, Laurel. Leave me alone."

He couldn't mean it. She laid her hand on his arm, closing her fingers over the taut muscles. "What do you want me to say?"

"That you love me. That you'll marry me."

"You're a dreamer, Cass," she said flatly, releasing her hold on him.

"Is that so bad?"

"It is if you don't see the reality around you," she answered. "We can never make our relationship permanent, and you know it."

"Do I?" he said stiffly.

"Yes, you do. You know I'm going back to Ohio in a few weeks, but you refuse to accept it."

"No," he replied. "You refuse to consider changing your plans."

"Well, what if I do? I'm a realist, not a princess in a fairy tale. Can you give me one good reason to change my mind?"

"I gave you the only reason you need, Laurel. I told you I love you."

"And that's supposed to fix everything? It won't, you know."

He stepped away from her and unrolled his sleeping bag on the floor. "It could be a start, if you'd let it," he said dryly.

Laurel went to her bedroom alone. Even Bear didn't seem to want to keep her company tonight. Well, she didn't care. Being alone was just fine with her if that was the way they wanted it.

She had resigned herself to the inevitable, and it was time Cass did the same. He would see things differently in the morning and begin to relish what little time they had, without making unreasonable demands on her. After sleeping on it, he would see.

Cass lay awake for hours before he could force himself to make the decision he knew he must. A doctor's degree was the kind of credential that would impress Laurel, but if he told her he'd never be sure if she loved Cass, the man, or Dr. John Cassidy, the astronomer with the Ph.D. If she couldn't love the man first, perhaps she never would.

There was no easy way out. He'd heard from Dave that Frank had left town. Laurel would be in no more danger. The longer he stayed, the harder it would be on both of them. Dawn hadn't yet broken when he rolled his sleeping bag, packed his gear, and left.

Love. A tear rolled silently down Laurel's cheek. Cass had said love would fix the whole mess. Sure it would, she thought cynically. Love was the cause of the conflict, not the solution. Instead of helping, it was forcing them apart, ruining everything. Damn love, she mouthed into the empty room before burying her face in her pillow to muffle the sobs of desperation. It was going to be a long night. She'd wait until morning and then try to reason with him. Cass had to see it her way. He had to.

Chapter Seven

Sunday, blessed Sunday, when the store was closed and she and Cass could stay home, enjoying each other's company. Laurel rolled over, rubbing the sleep from her eyes. It said seven on the bedside clock, but she heard no music or sounds of cooking. She smiled to herself. How predictable he was. She'd soon hear him come in from his walk, turn on the radio, and begin to prepare the breakfast he was so determined she needed. This morning, she'd eat whatever he fixed, without protest. Afterwards, they could calmly come to terms with their need for each other. Cass was bound to see it her way.

Stretching languidly, she lay on her back, thinking of their special times. The awful scene the night before made her realize all the more what a special man he was. Everything would be all right, if she didn't let him press her to deal with the end of their relationship. She sighed. This line of thinking was getting her down. She needed to get moving and pull her mind away from depressing thoughts of losing him.

Maybe, if she hurried, she could turn the tables and have his breakfast ready by the time he returned. The idea appealed to her. She would fix pancakes and sausage and surprise him.

Dressing quickly, Laurel hurried to the kitchen, gathered the necessary ingredients, and began making the batter while the sausage sizzled. Cass was late, but then it was Sunday. And where was Bear? Oh well, she thought, the two of them had undoubtedly gone for their walk the way they used to. The big dog had probably missed hiking with his master.

Turning the sausage for the third time, Laurel decided it was done and shut off the burner. It would be silly to heat the griddle until they had returned. The rest of the meal would keep. While she waited, she would straighten up the house. Damn, I feel domestic, she thought, smiling. The next thing I know, I'll be washing windows. Filling the sink with hot water and soap suds, she soaked the previous night's dishes. Housework wasn't so bad, she reasoned, when you had something to look forward to, like spending more time with Cass.

Laundry was next. Back in her room, Laurel gathered an armload of her clothes and stuffed them into the washer on the back porch. There was room for a few of Cass's shirts. He'd done his own laundry several days ago, but he was bound to have a dirty shirt or two by now. She had seen him stuff them in an outside compartment on his pack. Laurel decided to do him a favor and wash them. He always leaned his pack up against the back of the overstuffed armchair by the hearth.

WINTER'S PROMISE

Laurel peeked around the chair. That was funny. The pack wasn't there. Cass must have moved it. Maybe it was in the kitchen. Her brow furrowed. No, she would have fallen over it cooking breakfast if he had left it there. How strange. It was almost as if he had left.

She froze, her heart pounding in her throat. No. He couldn't, he wouldn't have left. She threw open the front door. "Bear," she called frantically, "Bear!" Leaving the door ajar, Laurel ran from room to room in the tiny house. There wasn't a sign that Cass had ever been there—nothing except the terrible sickness she felt, knowing he was gone.

Tears clouded her vision. They could have had two more weeks together. How could he leave?

Laurel leaned her back against the doorjamb. Now what? She could look for him or let him go. There was no real choice to make. She had to try to find him. Perhaps she could talk some sense into him, but if not at least she could feel his arms around her once again in a proper good-bye. Her body reacted to the thought of his touch with reckless excitement.

"Damn," she grumbled, wiping fresh tears off her cheeks.

Resolve replaced anguish as she pulled on a coat, grabbed her keys, locked the house, and started down the hill. "Think," she ordered herself. "Think. Where would he go? Which direction?" Cass had told her he had entered Julian past the museum. Chances were he would leave by one of the opposite routes. It was a long shot, but it was all she had to go on.

How far away could he be? Laurel shaded her eyes

with the flat of her hand and scanned the crossroads. She wouldn't have time to search both ways. Her choice had to be right the first time. With a deep breath and a half-sobbed sigh, she resolutely struck out for the highway to Borrego. The desert was coming into bloom, Sandy had told them, and Cass had expressed a wish to see it. Maybe . . .

The shape she saw ahead of the sloping roadway could have been almost anyone or anything, the distance was so great. Bright sun, shimmering off the asphalt, distorted her view. She had to get closer.

"This is the second time I've run in the last two days," she marveled, bouncing down the steep incline after the retreating apparition. Her pulse quickened. It looked like—it was! Bear rambled beside the man who trudged along before her.

"Cass! Wait!" Laurel called. The dog slowed his pace, but his master never faltered. "Cass!" Drat the man. He was determined to make her run after him like some star-struck groupie. Well, she'd come this far and she wasn't about to let him get away without an explanation. Not now.

The pitch of the hill increased. Laurel hadn't intended to run so fast, but her weight added to her momentum until she felt like she was flying. The weakness in her legs came on so suddenly, she had no time to stop. Then she was tumbling, unceremoniously, head over heels on the hard-packed, red clay shoulder of the winding highway. Her only thought, as she was falling, was that now she would never catch Cass. Stunned, she finally came to rest, sprawled like a rag doll.

WINTER'S PROMISE

Someone was shaking her gently. "Laurel," Cass called, "Laurel. Come on, open your eyes."

His body shaded her face. The blue sky framed his head, the sunshine making his hair and beard glow with a golden halo.

"Hmm," Laurel sighed, partially regaining her senses, "I didn't know angels had beards."

He straightened. "You're okay. Come on, Bear."

"I am *not* okay," she said, sitting up and holding her head. "If you leave me, you'll be responsible for abandoning an injured damsel."

Cass stopped short. "What did you say?"

Laurel was still rubbing her temples. "I'm hurt," she complained, "I'm not accountable for the things I say."

Dropping his pack, Cass sank to his knees next to her. "Here, let me see." He went over her from head to toe in a businesslike manner, his hands moving swiftly and surely. "You're fine as far as I can tell," he assured her. "But if you'd like, I'll flag down a car and try to get us a ride back to town to see a doctor."

"No," she said, "just let me rest a minute." His touch had been so formal and professional, she wondered if her efforts to find him had been wasted.

Cass crossed his legs and sat beside her on the edge of the roadway, staring into space.

It was now or never. Laurel was rapidly losing her nerve. "Why did you leave me?" she asked.

He gave an icy laugh. "I told you last night."

"No. You told me you loved me."

"And you said there was no hope for us. Do you enjoy torturing me, Laurel?"

"Of course not!" she exploded, "I just don't see why you can't stay until I leave for Ohio. We could have a great time together."

He shook his head. "Is that all you want from me—a great time? Sorry. I don't want to play games."

Games again. Perhaps that was the answer, she thought. Laurel poked him in the ribs, her fingers finding a ticklish spot. "Are you sure?" she teased, giggling.

"Stop that."

Launching herself at him, she dug her nails into the tender flesh under his arms.

"Stop tickling, you fiend," he chuckled, fighting to stay aloof and withdrawn. "I have a sensitive heart and soul, and all you want is my body."

"Well, mister," she laughed, still attacking, "you could stick around and prove to me how lovable you are."

Suddenly, his solemnity returned. He pried her hands loose, stood up, and shouldered his pack. "Goodbye, Laurel," he said quietly and started walking away.

He was leaving, really leaving. Laurel stood, her fists clenched, her body aching with wanting him, loving him, needing him. There was only one thing to do, her tormented heart cried out, before he was out of the range of her voice, her love. Do it, before it's too late. Do it. Tell him! "Damn it, Cassidy," she shouted after him, "I love you!"

In the silence that followed, it seemed even the birds were mute. Nothing stirred on the mountain.

Halting in mid-stride, Cass turned slowly to look back. His face was contorted, a reflection of unbearable pain. He stared at Laurel as new tears filled her eyes.

The question was unspoken, but crystal clear. She nodded, dropping her gaze, and saw his shadow cover hers as he walked back to her.

"Again," he said chokingly.

He had come back. Relief flooded over her. "I love you, Cassidy," she sobbed, "I love you."

Taking her in his arms, Cass held her close. "Thank you."

"For—for what?" she stammered.

"For giving us another chance," he replied tenderly. "Let's go home."

"You—you mean you'll stay?"

"I'd be a fool not to. I have two more weeks to convince you that you can't live without me."

Laurel was afraid her sobs might begin anew if she didn't lighten the mood. "You'll have your work cut out for you," she sniffed, "but I'm looking forward to having you try."

"You're insatiable," he laughed, squeezing her waist and pulling her to his side. "I hope I can survive two more weeks of your wanton seduction."

She poked her elbow in his ribs. "You'll muddle through, I'm sure."

"Is your world really so different?" Laurel asked as they walked slowly back to town, sharing a snack from Cass's pack. "I mean, isn't there some way we could . . . Oh, never mind," she shrugged, "I guess I'm just becoming a silly dreamer."

"That alone is a miracle," Cass observed. "A few days ago you didn't believe in dreams, remember?"

Laurel nodded in agreement. "It seems you've altered my thinking in a lot of ways, Cassidy."

"Are you sorry?"

She slipped her hand into his. "No," she said softly. "It's hard to explain, but I feel almost like a child, again. It's as if the last fifteen years never happened. There's a freedom to the whole thing that scares me."

Squeezing her hand, Cass waited, but she didn't continue. "Tell me more about your grandmother," he urged.

Laurel sighed audibly. "I don't remember much. I wish I did."

"What can you recall? Anything?"

"Only that she always had time for Steve and me." Laurel smiled at the memory. "She was very ill, but of course we weren't told. I suppose that made a difference in her priorities, in the way she viewed the world. No matter what she was doing, she always stopped to listen, or tell us stories, or sing to us."

"She sang?"

"Uh huh. Folk songs, mostly. You know, the kind that told stories. I've often tried to remember them, but all I get are bits and pieces."

Minutes passed before Laurel spoke again. "I guess the thing I remember most, though, is her kindness. Steve and I would snuggle up to her, one on each side, and she'd hug us while she knitted or read or sang those fascinating old songs."

Cass was thoughtfully watching Laurel's reactions.

"What did your grandmother look like?" he asked quietly.

"I wish I knew. All the old photos have been lost or destroyed."

"Honey, that's not true," Cass said. "I'm standing here with the picture of her love. Don't you see? You're what it produced and nurtured, and I love her for giving so much of herself to you."

"She would have liked you, too, Cass," Laurel said, shaking her head from side to side. "You're a nut, but a thoroughly enchanting one. She'd have had you in her kitchen, stirring a big pot of strawberry jam and listening to her stories, before you had hardly said hello."

"Sounds like a fun lady."

"She was. Come on." Laurel tugged his hand. "Let's get going before I get weepy again."

Cass smiled. "How about a little detour? You didn't leave anything on the stove, did you?"

"Nope. I started to prepare breakfast, but when I realized you were gone, I left the whole, cold mess sitting in the sink. It'll probably look pretty awful by the time we get home. To tell you the truth, it didn't look great when it was fresh." She giggled.

"That's okay. Come on."

"Wait a minute," Laurel gasped breathlessly as she followed him off the road and up a steep hill. "Where are we going?"

"My world, or at least a small part of it. I promise, if you don't like it, we'll head straight for Julian. Give me a half a chance?"

Catching up, Laurel panted heavily. "If I live that long."

He took her hand. "Look at all the wild flowers, Laurel. The tall, blue spikes over there are lupine, and those lush green bushes are from the gooseberry family."

"Well, I once pictured you living off nuts and berries. You haven't disappointed me."

His hand tightened around hers. "I hope I never do," he whispered. "Laurel, there's something—"

"Look!" she interrupted him as they crested a low rise. "What're those? There must be a million of them. Oh, Cass, they're beautiful!"

Purple blankets of tiny flowers covered the sunlit ridges ahead of them. "Those are milk vetch," Cass explained. "Every winter, this place is barren, but, come spring, these hills are aglow with beauty and color." He searched her eyes, turning her to face him. "Don't you see?" he asked. "It's a promise that's always kept. Winter's promise. It's a renewal of life, full of the most marvelous surprises, and it comes just when it seems that all the good has died."

"You've missed your calling," Laurel said uncomfortably. "You should have been a philosopher or a preacher."

"Sorry. Sometimes I get carried away."

"That's okay," she laughed. "At least if you kill me on this endurance marathon of yours, I know you'll have some flowery words to say over my grave."

Stooping, she plucked a bright yellow dandelion. "Here you go. How's this for romantic? The universal weed, found coast to coast, and the plague of every gardener."

Cass chuckled. "It's like people, Laurel. The beauty is in the eye of the beholder. If you hadn't prejudged it, what would you say about it?"

She looked closely at the small yellow flower with its sticky white sap clinging in droplets to her fingers. There was a delicate beauty to it, after all. "I—I guess I may have unfairly maligned the poor little thing," she admitted.

"Good," Cass replied, "that's a start. Now, when you can look at people, especially me, with that much honesty, maybe we'll have a chance."

"You never give up, do you?" she asked, dropping the flower.

"Nope. Not now." Cass paused. "You haven't suddenly decided to discard me the way you did the dandelion, have you?"

She looked longingly into his eyes as her hand lightly cupped his cheek and beard. "No," she whispered, "I still love you to the point of idiocy."

Bending slowly, Cass joined his lips to hers tenderly, yet passionately.

Her arms tried to wind around his neck to bring him closer, but the frame of the backpack interferred.

"We seem to have a problem," Cass teased, "but I'm afraid if I take the pack off, I may be tempted to make love to you right here."

"Mmm," Laurel purred, still caressing his face with her lips, "sounds better all the time."

With both hands on her shoulders, Cass leaned her away from him. "No, love. Not here. You're irresistible,

I admit, but believe me, the ants, flies, and leaves do little for the libido."

Laurel opened her dreamy eyes and glared, half teasing, half serious. "Oh? And how would you know?" she demanded.

Grinning, he gave her a resounding wack on the bottom. "Somebody told me, of course. Now, come on. The sooner we get home, the sooner you can begin to seduce me again."

"Ooh! You're awful. You make me sound like a cross between Salome and Mata Hari."

Laughing, Cass corrected her. "Oh, no, Laurel. I had in mind something more like half angel, half shameless hussy."

"You're a mean man, Cassidy," she shot back.

"But lovable," he added. "Don't forget lovable."

She squeezed his hand. "And lovable," she agreed, "very lovable. Take me home."

Cass laughed again. "I feel like the kid who comes home with a puppy and says, 'It followed me home. Can I keep it?'"

Laurel jabbed her elbow in his ribs, laughing with him, and nearly stepped into a slowly flowing stream.

Tiny brown fish, some no bigger than a small insect, darted through the rippling water, hiding beneath floating debris.

"This is the Mississippi, I take it," Laurel teased.

"No, the Amazon. Look out for those piranha."

"Sure, Cassidy, sure. You just want me to leap into your arms for protection, don't you?"

He laughed heartily. "Sounds good to me. Come to think of it, I've heard it has crocodiles, too."

"That does it," she said, placing her hands on his shoulders. Touching the tip of her nose to the end of his, she looked him straight in the eye. "I don't believe you."

Cass grabbed playfully for her as she stepped quickly away. His trained eye absently watched her path as she walked on ahead of him.

Suddenly, he was running. "Laurel!" Her name became a gutteral exclamation just before he reached her, spinning her around and knocking her off balance.

Wide-eyed, she saw the terror plainly written on his face. "Wh—what happened?"

Concentrating on a pile of leaves several yards away, Cass pointed. "Snake," he said, then relaxed almost immediately. "It's okay. It's not a rattler."

"A—a rattlesnake? Here?"

"No, not this time," Cass said. "I should have realized it was too early in the season and too cold. Seeing that gopher snake really suprises me. None of them should be active yet either."

"Oh, swell," Laurel said, teasingly. "First piranha then crocodiles, and now rattlesnakes."

"That's why I didn't yell for you to freeze. We'd been kidding so much about imaginary dangers, I figured you'd think I was joking and keep right on walking."

"I suppose I would have," she decided realistically. "Thanks. Even if it wasn't a rattlesnake, you thought it was. I guess that counts as a real rescue." A shiver shot down her spine at the thought.

Cass wrapped her protectively in his arms. "It's okay now, love."

Nestled warmly against his chest, Laurel basked in the feeling of belonging and all her fears vanished. "When you hold me close," she murmured, "I feel like I could take on the whole world and win."

"Even this wilderness I've brought you to?" he asked quietly.

"Even your wilderness." She sighed deeply.

He held her away from him, his hands firmly gripping her upper arms. "No, Laurel. It was foolish to bring you up here without some advance preparation. It's too dangerous for a beginner. I'm sorry."

"Don't be silly."

Cass shuddered almost imperceptibly. "It's not silly. I could've gotten you hurt." His fingers tightened on her arms. "Good Lord, I could've killed you in my selfish desire to show you the beauties of the mountains." Color drained from his face.

Laurel reached up to his forehead, her fingertips smoothing the furrowed lines of his brow. "But you didn't." She stood on tiptoe, her lips brushing his in a kiss of forgiveness and understanding. "It's all right. Really. I do think the country is lovely."

He cupped her upturned face in his hands. "The loveliest thing up here is you, Laurel," he said softly. "The flowers are nothing in comparison."

"You're just prejudiced."

"You're right." Cass's eyes met hers, holding their bodies hypnotized in the magic of the understanding passing between them. Finally, he broke the bond of oneness. "Let's go home."

Laurel's face was still lifted to meet his. "Kiss me, first?"

"With pleasure," he agreed, bringing his lips gently to hers. The sparks smoldering just beneath the surface threatened to leap into an all-consuming fire once again.

Arching toward him, Laurel melted into his kiss, the love and desire that had been in her gaze moments before unmistakably enveloping her body.

Cass's breathing was labored as he pushed her away. "No. Not here. Not like this."

She looked at him openly. "Why?"

"Because I want it to be perfect between us," he said hoarsely. "Always."

Laurel lowered her lashes and let herself be led down the mountain while thoughts of her uncertain future flashed through her tormented mind. He had said "Always," as if he expected their love to last forever.

Julian was still fairly crowded with weekend tourists when she and Cass reached Washington and Main Streets.

By the side of an old brick building, a man was photographing his wife beside the historical data painted on the wall. "Say, folks," he said to Cass and Laurel, "would you mind snapping this for me so I can get in the picture, too?"

"No problem," Cass said genially. "How does your camera work?"

"Simple," the man explained. "You just look through here, push the button, and the camera spits out the picture."

Obligingly, Cass took several shots for the visitors.

"Now," the man said to Cass, "how about one of you and your missus? It'd be my way of thankin' you."

Cass drew Laurel against his side before she could protest. "For a keepsake," he said lightly. "Smile."

They were home before the picture finished developing itself. Holding it gingerly by the white margin, Laurel watched as Cass's beaming face became more defined. He looked so ludicrously happy. And she? The camera had caught her looking up at him lovingly, and Laurel thought she could see the sadness she had felt when he had suggested the photo as a keepsake. It was. Carefully, she tucked the precious picture in with her personal belongings. The time would most certainly come when the snapshot would be all she had left to remind her of the one man she'd been able to love, the one man she would never be able to forget. It was a small token, but at least it was something.

Startled, Laurel jumped when he entered the room. Slamming the bureau drawer, she turned to face him.

"Secrets already?" he asked.

"I—I was just putting the picture way."

"Photos are nice, my love, but you have the real thing."

Cass crossed the room and was so close she could feel his breath whispering along her skin. All day she had wanted him. Partway through the afternoon, when he'd held her and kissed her amid the fields of spring flowers, she had seriously considered saying to hell with the ants and leaves and propositioning him there in the wooded seclusion of the hills. She looked longingly up at him, her lips soft and slightly parted.

"This is one of those times when I see the angel in you," Cass said quietly.

Expecting his kiss, she leaned closer.

"Did you have a good time today?" he asked, resting his hands on her shoulders.

Laurel nodded, stepping closer. Her long lashes brushed against his beard, and her touch at his waist was an intimate, unconscious caress.

Cass's hands framed her face, his fingers working into her thick auburn hair and tightening. "My God, Laurel," he rasped, "do you have any idea how hard it was to leave you?"

"Then why . . . ?"

"I've asked myself the same thing," he said. Pausing, he drew her closer. "Methinks we philosophize too much," he joked in paraphrase. "Come here, angel."

"How about the shameless hussy part?" she drawled. Pushing her body against the length of his, she succeeded in fitting her curves into his muscular angles.

"That luscious body of yours has taunted me all day," he whispered. "I almost took you in the woods, in spite of the lack of comfort."

"We could have saved a lot of time," Laurel giggled, "because I was thinking the same thing."

"Do you think I didn't know that? When you snuggled up to me after we saw the snake, I almost lost control."

"I wish you had," she said, blushing slightly. She remembered the previous night and his unwillingness to make love to her. He seemed to have so much control, perhaps he wasn't as much in love as she was.

The doubt was mirrored in her expression, and Cass read it clearly. He looked into her eyes, the smile fading from his face as his brow furrowed. "Say it again," he pleaded. "Say you love me."

This was no time for teasing. Laurel sensed the hold she had on him now, but she also knew the agony in his voice was no act. He needed to hear her confess her love and she couldn't deny him. Loving him had become the most important thing in her life, even if it was only to be a short-lived ecstasy. "I love you, Cass," she whispered hoarsely, "with every ounce of strength and every thought."

His lips descended on hers, crushing her softness in an unspoken plea for proof.

Laurel moaned with the pleasurable pain and returned the urgent kiss with total abandon. Her body pressed against his in a writhing yearning for the completed love only he could provide.

Cass's hands traced the curve of her spine and caressed the roundness of her hips before he clasped her tightly to him. "Laurel," he groaned, his face buried in her wavy auburn tresses, "I need you."

"And you still love me?" she groped wishfully.

He raised his head and looked deeply into her eyes, "Forever," he whispered roughly. "No matter what."

Laurel knew that was also true of her love for him. This interlude had already changed her as a person, and she had no doubt it would affect her the rest of her life. With great difficulty, she forced her thoughts back to the present. The future would take care of itself. She couldn't afford to waste their brief time

WINTER'S PROMISE

together worrying about something over which she had no control.

Trembling, her fingers began to unfasten the buttons on his soft flannel shirt. "I need you, too," she whispered. Her cheek brushed the tantalizing coarseness of his beard as she lowered her lips to trace his collarbone with feathery kisses before she bent to explore the fine, curly hairs covering his bare chest.

A rumbling moan echoed through him. Almost savagely, Cass grabbed the waist of her sweater and jerked it over her head, tossing it to the floor. His hands fumbled momentarily with the clasp on her bra before that, too, was eliminated. He caressed her soft breasts with the palms of his hands, his thumbs teasing her nipples erect.

Laurel dug her nails into the muscles of his shoulders. "Cass, don't," she begged.

"Why not? You like it, don't you?"

"You're driving me crazy," she gasped.

"Then do something about it," he said breathlessly.

Her hands flew to his belt, undoing the buckle and tearing futilely at the button beneath.

Cass curved one arm around her shoulders and bent to place the other under her knees, lifting her swiftly into his arms and striding across the room.

Laurel kept her arms clasped tightly around his neck as he lowered her onto the colorful, quilted bedspread.

He gently loosened her grasp. "You'll have to let me go for a second, love," he said quietly.

She watched in fascination as he finished the job she had bungled in her urgency. His want was as evident as her own and through her passion-dazed mind, Laurel realized that his body was the most beautiful thing she had ever seen. Stretching out her arms to him, she wove her fingers into the hair at his temples while Cass knelt by her and slowly unfastened her jeans, placing a tingling kiss on her taut abdomen.

"They were right," Laurel moaned in ecstasy.

"Who?" Cass asked, his voice muffled by the bare skin he was caressing with his gentle, butterfly kisses.

Laurel lifted her hips for him. "The women who liked your beard," she groaned. "It tickles and sets me on edge at the same time."

"Good," he whispered. Removing the rest of her clothes, Cass let his eyes travel deliciously over her.

How could he stand to be so close yet so far? She reached for him again, pulling his head down between her breasts.

Cass kissed the rounded softness, letting his hand follow her curves, over her abdomen, to the center of her desire.

"Damn you, Cassidy," she rasped, "you're the meanest tease in the world."

In a moment, he was over her, his weight pressing her struggling body to the bed. "You mean you've had enough?"

"Never," she agonized as her body arched into his. "I'll never get enough of you." Laurel parted her thighs, opening herself to him as a flower opens to the morning sun. "Please!"

"Oh, Laurel, my love." Cass joined them, his whole

body trembling in the effort to be gentle despite his overpowering need.

Laurel closed her eyes, her hands clutching his back, feeling his muscles' fluid rhythm as he moved over her. He literally took her breath away, and she let herself drown in the magnificent euphoria surrounding them.

Time and again Cass built her desire almost to its peak, then let it ebb ever so slightly until she was so exhausted she thought she couldn't go on. Their bodies gleamed, flesh sliding against flesh effortlessly, smoothly.

"Do you still want me?" he gasped.

Laurel nodded vigorously, digging her nails into his shoulders.

"Then, you'll have me," he moaned, driving hard against her with a surging, primitive rhythm.

She raised herself to his loving assault and heard him groan as she muffled her cries against his lips.

Slowly, their passion cooled and their tired muscles began to relax. Cass rolled to one side, bringing Laurel with him in his arms. He was still out of breath. "Whew! You wear me out."

Snuggling closer, Laurel asked, "Am I too hard to please?"

He squeezed her. "No, You're too hard to resist. The tiring part is trying to hold back. I don't want to cheat you."

Laurel giggled. "Who's keeping score?"

"If I don't impress you with my romantic skill," he joked glibly, "what do I have left?" He was silent for a few seconds, then went on. "I suppose I could go out, enroll in college, and start amassing those degrees that mean so much to you."

Was he serious? Laurel held her breath. "Would you?"

"If I did, love, it would have to be because that was what I wanted for myself."

"Not because of me?"

"No," he said slowly. "A man has his pride, Laurel. I wouldn't be worth having if I had no mind of my own."

She had to agree, at least to herself. Part of Cass's charm was his strength of character. Still, if he was willing to kid around about adopting her life-style, maybe he'd been giving it some serious thought. It was a possibility, the only one Laurel had been able to grasp so far, and she clung to the idea hopefully.

Chapter Eight

Waking each morning in Cass's arms was beginning to feel so natural that Laurel found it hard to remember her life any other way. Murmuring softly, she snuggled closer, reveling in his presence—the touch of his skin, the fine, curly hairs on his arms and legs, the strength of his beloved body, the gentleness of his caring.

He kissed the hairline on her forehead. "Morning."

"Umm. I like it here. Let's skip morning."

"Nope, not today," he replied.

A little more awake, Laurel tried to place the day. "It's Sunday again, isn't it?" She felt a warm glow. They had belonged to each other for a whole week.

"Mm hmm," he answered. "How would you like to walk up to church this morning?"

Her eyes popped open and she raised herself on one elbow, staring at him. "Church?" she squeaked. "Whatever for?"

"Why not?"

"Well, because . . ." she let her words trail off, obviously embarrassed.

"Because we've been living together?" he guessed, grinning.

Laurel was silent. It wasn't funny. She might be living in liberated times, but her roots went deep and so did the ideas she was taught as a child.

"It's okay, Laurel," he said. "Their sign says, 'Come as you are.'"

"Dummy," she scolded, "that's clothing, not lifestyle."

Cass laughed warmly. "Don't be so sure. If all the people who went to church were perfect, they'd have no reason to go."

She shook her head. "You're unbelievable, Cassidy. You have an answer for everything, don't you?"

"I hope so."

"It's been a long time since I went anywhere like church," she said pensively.

"And I'll bet your grandmother was the one who took you, right?"

Laurel looked at him in surprise. "All right, Cassidy, where's your crystal ball and turban?"

He waited patiently for her to continue.

Lying back on the fluffy pillow, she stared at the ceiling. "I remember it like it was yesterday," she mused. "Gram held my hand and led me into this enormous room full of friendly people. The stained glass windows glowed like rainbows and the smooth wooden pews vibrated when the organ played the hymns." She hesitated. "It was a good time. A happy time."

"Good. Then it's settled," he concluded. "We can have breakfast and still make the later service."

"You're serious!"

"Always," he replied with a smile. Throwing back the covers, he left her and headed for the bathroom.

Laurel heard the shower start. Church. The man was one surprise after another. She couldn't help wondering if he had some ulterior motive for suggesting they attend the service together. In the glorious hours of the past week, he hadn't once brought up the subject of marriage or commitment. Perhaps this was his way of slipping the idea into her mind again. A church wedding. How she wished it could be so. Why do I have to be such a pragmatic realist? she agonized. Why can't I see myself free as a butterfly, let go, and fly? I wish I'd never gone to college, she thought in abject misery. But I've seen the other world, my world, and my place is there. Nothing can change that. I have a responsible position, and a duty not to waste the expertise I fought so hard to gain. I could run from my job or my career, but I'd never escape myself. Nor should I try, she added glumly. I am what I am.

And Cass? Laurel sat on the edge of the cold and lonely bed. Cass. She folded her arms across her chest, hugging herself to stop the horrible, empty longing. Love was supposed to be wonderful, and when they were together it was. But what about later? One more week of bliss remained. One more week of belonging, then nothing.

The water stopped splattering against the shower walls.

"Hey, Laurel," Cass called, "you'd better hurry, or you'll miss your big chance to rub my back."

He sounded so happy. She had to stop thinking about what was to come or she knew she'd spoil the rest of their time. Slipping off her gown, Laurel started toward the steamy bathroom. "You're not fooling me, Cassidy," she said with forced gaiety. "It's not your back you want rubbed, is it?"

A booming, joyful laugh echoed through the half open door. "You've a touch of the fortune teller in you, love," he countered. "And what would you like rubbed?"

Only Laurel's sense of propriety kept her from leaving in the middle of the church service when the minister began speaking about commitment. Nervously, she smoothed her wool skirt, her glance darting to Cass in his jeans and plaid shirt.

Becoming aware of her uneasiness, he took her hand in his, holding it reassuringly throughout the rest of the sermon.

She heard little more of the sermon. Her mind was churning, along with her stomach. Dear Lord, she thought, almost as a prayer, what am I going to do without him?

Cass squeezed her hand as they filed out of the old clapboard church with the rest of the congregation.

Children in their Sunday best sought out their parents and loudly announced what they had learned in Sunday school.

For the first time in her life, Laurel envied parents. Somehow, along with so many other new things, children had also become desirable.

Cass patted her hand. He had been watching her

as she looked fondly at the youngsters. "I can fix you right up," he volunteered, leading the way down the hill, away from the crowd.

"What?"

"I think we should have at least four," he went on, "two boys and two girls."

"Oh, sure," Laurel shot back. "And we can get them tiny pink and blue backpacks while we drag them all over the country. Uh uh." The thought of having his children tied her stomach in knots of yearning, and she felt an unaccountable anger rising inside.

"I do think we should get married first," Cass said matter-of-factly. "Kids need a stable environment."

That was the last straw. "Stable environment!" she snapped. "What do you know about stability?" Even the hurt look on his face wasn't enough to stop her tirade. Everything she had been saving spilled out. "A man who goes roaming all over the country is no example of stability. You only lit here because I was in a jam. Otherwise you'd have been long gone." She didn't mean to say the next thing on her mind, but her unleashed anger overrode her more sensible thoughts. "Well, you don't have to worry anymore," she continued. "Frank left town two days after we caught him in the house." Laurel bit her lip. Why, oh why, had she told him? There was nothing more she could say. The damage was done.

Cass looked at her with an unreadable expression. "I know," he said. "I've known all along."

Her eyes widened incredulously. So that was why he hadn't been worried about her safety when he'd left.

"The trouble was," he said quietly, "I'd already come to care for you by then."

Wordlessly, they continued down the hill. When they were almost to the house, Cass spoke again. "Marry me, Laurel."

She couldn't answer. The words she wanted to say caught in her throat. Marrying him was what she longed for, but it was impossible to resolve their other problems. In bed, they were totally compatible, but there was more to marriage than just a good sexual adjustment.

"Please?"

Don't beg, damn it, she thought, her ire building. It's hard enough as it is.

"Laurel?"

"Stop it, Cassidy," she nearly shouted, "just stop it!"

"Talk to me, Laurel. Tell me why. Put it into words so we can discuss it."

"No. You want to belabor a point that only has one possible result. You're trying to get me to talk myself into a marriage I know is doomed to failure. When I do get married, Cass, I intend it to be forever."

His voice was so quiet, she almost didn't hear his reply.

"So do I."

Openmouthed, Laurel stared after him as he entered the house. She sank to the porch steps, pulling her knees up under her chin. Now what? Would they be able to return to the easygoing relationship they'd shared for the past seven days? Laurel doubted it.

A distant jangle stirred her. The phone rang twice,

then stopped. Curious, she made her way into the living room.

"Yes," Cass was saying, "this is."

With his back to the door, he hadn't seen her come in.

"Yes," he said crisply, "she is, but she's unable to get to the phone right now. Perhaps I can help you." The shouting from the other end of the line caused Cass to hold the receiver away from his ear.

Across the room, Laurel could, unfortunately, hear some of the words. "Here," she said, reaching for the instrument.

Eyebrows raised, Cass handed her the phone and stepped back.

"This is Laurel Phillips," she began. In a moment, she had discovered the identity of her caller. "Rob! It's great to hear from you. How's Joan?"

"Never mind that," Rob demanded. "Who's the guy?"

"A friend."

"A friend who answers your phone on Sunday morning?" Rob asked pointedly. "How convenient."

"My friends are my business," Laurel replied, her heart pounding irrationally in its reaction to Rob's accusing tone.

"And my business?" he went on. "How is *my* business?"

"Fine," she assured him. "Receipts are even up a little over last month's."

"Good." Rob's voice was losing some of its surliness. "Listen, Laurel, I'm sorry I got so hot with you. It's not that I don't trust you, it's just that I've had my finger on the pulse of that store for so long it's in my blood. You understand, don't you?"

Laurel was able to control the nervous waver in her voice. "Of course. No problem."

"Good. Now, one more thing. I was talking to a fellow down here who does some meat exporting and I'd like to keep the connection open, but I need some figures from Frank to firm up the deal. I'll give you my phone number and you tell Frank to give me a call in the morning. Okay?"

Oh dear. This was getting sticky. There was no way Laurel could have contacted Frank, had she wanted to, and she certainly had no desire to do that. She had no choice but to tell Rob.

Taking a deep breath, to calm her trembling body, she began. "Rob, I don't know quite how to tell you this. Frank doesn't work for you anymore." The silence was so pure, Laurel wondered if the line had gone dead. "Rob?"

"What happened?" he asked stiffly.

She could almost see his clenched teeth. "I fired him."

"You *what*? Oh, I get it. You canned the best manager I've ever had and replaced him with your boyfriend. Is that it?"

He was right about the result. How was she going to prove he was wrong about her motives, especially over the phone?

She had to try. "Listen, Rob, it's not like that at all," she explained. Silence. "Rob? Rob?"

A soft, feminine voice answered her. "Laurel, honey," Joan said, "what's happened?"

WINTER'S PROMISE

Laurel sighed. "It's a long story, Joan. Frank made a pass at me and I fired him."

"And the other guy?" her friend probed.

"The other guy and I are shacking up," Laurel said dryly, slipping into the vulgar euphemism with little regard for her upbringing, "and I don't give a damn what Rob thinks."

"Whoa, Laurel. This is Joan, your pal, remember? You don't have to get defensive with me."

"Sorry, it's been a rough morning." Laurel ran her fingers through her hair, pushing it off her forehead.

"So I gathered. Apparently this whole business has been rough on you. Hold on, Laurel, Rob wants to tell me something."

A muffled noise led Laurel to believe her friend had placed a hand over the mouthpiece.

"Uh, Laurel," Joan began, "Rob says we're coming home."

Blankly, Laurel listened to the message from Rob. He had decided to cut their stay short and return to salvage what he could of the business he thought Laurel had sabotaged. He wanted Cass gone when he got there. "I'm sorry, Joan," she told the other woman. "Your vacation won't be as nice as you'd thought."

"Honey," Joan said, "Rob has been itching to get home since we arrived. Coming back to Julian may very well save my sanity. Don't worry, okay?"

"Okay," Laurel said, without feeling. Joan's goodbye was followed by a loud click.

Cass was watching her. "Rob, of Rob's Market, I take it."

Laurel nodded, her hair falling forward to sweep

over her cheeks and hide her misery. Rob had effectively killed the relationship between her and Cass without even knowing it.

She felt the sensitive touch she had grown to adore as Cass put his arm around her shaking shoulders. "They're coming home?"

"Yes."

"When?"

"As soon as Rob can change their flight. They should be here no later than tomorrow evening. He said he wants you gone by then."

"Then we have tonight," Cass said gently. "Unless you've reconsidered my proposal."

"No." The word came out far more forcefully than she had intended.

"I thought not," he said icily. "You're all fun and games, aren't you, Laurel?"

"It wasn't *me* who asked you to go away. This is Rob's house. Don't be cruel."

"Cruel? Lady, you take the prize for that one."

"I never lied to you," she whispered. "Never. I always told you there was no chance for us."

"You got so used to saying it, you refused to see any other alternative, didn't you? You had your nice, warm, bed partner with no strings attached. Right?"

"Stop it!"

"I almost gagged when you said we were shacking up," he railed. "Is that all it's been to you, Laurel? Some sordid little interlude to write in your diary?"

"No!" she exclaimed, a telltale sob in her voice. More quietly, "No." Turning away, she fought the tears gathering in her eyes.

His hands touched her upper arms, tentatively, tenderly. "I'm sorry, Laurel," he whispered against her hair. "I was out of line."

That was too much. His anger was much easier to deal with. Laurel's shoulders began to shake and she buried her face in her hands.

Cass turned her toward him.

"I'm sorry, too."

Folding her in his arms, Cass bowed his head over hers, and his quiet tears fell, unheeded, to mingle with her hair.

Dinner that evening was returned to the refrigerator almost untouched.

Cass apologized as he stacked the dishes. "I guess I wasn't very hungry."

"Me, either," Laurel replied. "How about a fire in the fireplace? We could sit by it and talk."

"Sure." The pile of wood on the hearth was almost gone and Cass went outside to replenish it.

Sighing deeply, Laurel settled into the corner of the couch and affectionately watched as he laid the fire and lit it. He had suggested they talk, earlier, but Laurel hadn't been ready to then. There was something she needed to tell him. It might not help the overall picture, but she knew he deserved to know what he meant to her.

Cass joined her. "You wanted to talk?"

"I need to know you understand, before—before—"

"Before it's over?"

She nodded sadly. "It isn't, it wasn't, sordid."

"No, love, it wasn't," he whispered, taking her

hand. He had come to the point where it no longer mattered what her reasons were for loving him. It was time to confess the truth he had been hiding, to let her know they could be together, after all. "Laurel, I want to tell you—"

"Wait," she interrupted, "I've rehearsed this in my head all afternoon. Let me say it. Please."

His eyes focused on her with love and patience. "Okay, you first."

"I want you to know I've been totally truthful with you," she began. "I do love you—more than I ever dreamed was possible—and I know you've been honest in return."

"Laurel, I—"

"It's all right, Cass, really. You've taught me so much about love and life and being a real person. My life has changed completely. You're a wonderful man and you've earned my respect for both you and your ideals. I'll treasure them always." She reached into the pocket of her beige silk blouse, producing a neatly lettered card. "Here."

Cass took the card.

"It's my address and phone number in Ohio," she explained unnecessarily. "I know you have no place to call home, but I was hoping you'd try to keep in touch." Her steady voice seemed to waver slightly. "Will you? Please?"

He nodded in agreement, placing the card in his wallet. "Laurel, you know I love you, don't you?"

"Of course," she said softly.

"Sometimes, things—well, things aren't what they seem."

"I know that," Laurel said. "Since losing my grandmother, you're the only person I've felt I could trust enough to love. You're very special to me, Cassidy. You've changed my whole outlook on life." She paused. "Now, there was something you wanted to say?"

"Maybe later," he mumbled, leaning back and staring into the leaping flames. "But maybe never."

Laurel shifted to her knees on the couch and lowered her body across his lap, facing him. "You could just hold me," she suggested nervously, afraid he might not want her physically.

Strong arms cradled her against his chest. "No matter what happens, remember that my love will always be there for you. It won't change," he said haltingly.

Dear Cass. He was obviously trying to prepare her for a future where only the memory of their love remained. Tonight, Laurel determined she'd be strong. Tonight, there'd be no recriminations, no weeping, no sadness. Laurel had steeled herself all day against the feelings of this moment. She would be fine. To carry this off without tears would help convince Cass he hadn't ruined her life, but instead had enriched it beyond words. There would be time enough later to cry—alone.

"I think I'll be your shameless hussy tonight," she said with feigned lightness. "You interested?" Laurel switched off the lamp and held her breath. He looked so serious, she was afraid she couldn't reach far enough into his black mood to break it.

Cass gazed at her pale, glowing face, those beautiful,

bewitching eyes begging him to respond. She deserved a proper good-bye, a night beyond forgetting. Then, when he did gain the courage to tell her the truth about himself, perhaps she could be persuaded to forgive him. He brought his lips down to hers in a gentle, searching kiss. There would be plenty of time to tell her, afterward, when her problems with Rob and the store were settled. He would fly to Ohio, if necessary, and bring her back. Cass only hoped she would have him.

Laurel melted into his kiss, pressing her firm breasts against him, one arm thrown around his neck, the other circling his waist.

"I'm interested," Cass whispered. "What did you have in mind?"

"Oh, maybe a little harmless seduction."

A smile raised the edges of his mustache. "There's nothing harmless about your seduction, love," he said quietly. "You are definitely a dangerous lady."

"Scared?" she taunted.

"Terrified."

She drew the nail of her index finger along his jaw to the point of his chin, twisting little curls in his beard. "Good," she drawled. Her fingers slid down to the buttons on his shirt, slowly opening one after the other until she could slip her hand inside and caress his bare skin.

"Mmm," Cass moaned. "I'm still scared. You'd better kiss me to calm me down."

Laurel giggled, her hand creeping around his neck under his collar. "Poor Cass." Raising herself slightly, she sought his eager lips.

WINTER'S PROMISE

Their kiss deepened. Then, suddenly, Cass pulled away, a sly smile on his lips.

"You're teasing me," Laurel observed correctly.

He cocked one eyebrow. "Maybe. What are you going to do about it?"

So, he wanted to tease, did he? Well, two could play that game, she thought. Slowly, sensuously, Laurel slid out of his arms, climbed off the couch, and stood before him, the fire at her back. Stripping for a man was new to her, but then so was most everything else she and Cass had experienced together.

Laurel slipped off her shoes, then her belt. Letting her wool skirt slide sensuously over her hips to fall to the floor, she paused, her eyes searching Cass's face. She wanted to please him, to arouse him, but she didn't want him to think she was well practiced at what she was doing. This was just for him.

He smiled, and Laurel could see his breathing growing more rapid.

"Not too much for you, is it?" she taunted sweetly.

Holding out his hand to her, Cass was surprised when she stepped farther away.

"I'm not done," she whispered, reaching for the buttons on her blouse. Her hands trembled so, she was afraid she might not be able to manage the simple task. Finally, the silk slid smoothly off her shoulders to fall in a heap on the floor.

Moments later, she stood before him in the wispy beige lace of her bra and panties. The fire lit her skin to a glowing ivory, and her hair was a halo of burnished gold and ruby.

"Dear God, Laurel," Cass pleaded, "that's enough."

He sat on the edge of the couch, reaching for her. "Come here, before I go crazy." The reflection of the fire's flames danced in his eyes.

In two steps, she was standing directly in front of him. She could feel his hot breath on the bare skin of her midriff just before he kissed her there, wrapping his arms around her and nuzzling his beard against her tender abdomen. Laurel was in heaven, lost in the magical essence of the moment.

Her bra fell away quickly as his practiced fingers released the clasp, then hooked in the lace of her briefs and stripped them from her.

Laurel wound her fingers into his hair, drawing his face against her body once more. Never had his mouth been so plundering, so desirable.

Cass's hands explored the soft curves of her back as his rough kisses intensified her deep, throbbing longing.

Weak from the feverish exhilaration, Laurel slowly knelt, her lips seeking his, her arms wrapped tightly around his neck. "Oh, Cass," Laurel gasped against the coarseness of his beard as he reached for the buckle of his belt. The teasing was over. She needed him with an intensity that left no place for hesitation.

Her slow, fumbling efforts were more than Cass could stand. He fastened his hands over hers. "Stay right there," he breathed raggedly, standing to finish removing his clothes.

The firelight bathed him in the same glow that had highlighted Laurel, and she saw his nude body gleam, his obvious need sending a thrill of desire coursing through her.

WINTER'S PROMISE

Cass returned to the couch, pulling her down with him.

Resting her cheek on his chest, Laurel savored the sound of his rapidly pounding heart. He wanted her as much as she wanted him, this marvelous man she loved so completely.

Lifting gently, Cass urged her up and over him, her thighs lying searingly against his.

All feelings of impropriety vanished in the flaring excitement surrounding them. The most sensitive part of her was pressed tightly to him in a warm, welcoming kiss of desire.

An almost soundless groan of passion escaped him. Cass slid beneath her, his hands possessively grasping her hips, his body desperately searching for the depths of her fire.

Laurel's urgency matched his own, and she embraced him sensuously, tightly, with every fiber of her being, as they came together. He took her breath away. She cried out, her fingernails biting into his shoulders.

Cass's hands held jealously to her hips while his lips were free to explore the softness of her breasts, raining feathery kisses round and round until he reached each peak. Taking her gently in his mouth, his tongue drove Laurel delirious with joy.

"Ahh" she moaned, writhing against him, "do something, please."

Gripping her tighter, he whispered, "I am," as he raged against her with a primitive lust, raising them both to the zenith of throbbing rapture. "Now!" Cass groaned. The intensity of the moment washed over her in waves of excruciating pleasure, tearing a cry from her lips at the moment of his ultimate possession.

Laurel fought for air, her chest heaving against Cass's. His grip was so tight! "Cass," she gasped, "I—I can't breathe!"

Very slowly, his arms released her and she began to relax. Perspiration trickled from his forehead, successfully masking the few tears that stole from his closed eyes.

He looked so young, lying there like that. Laurel let her hands drift softly over his heaving chest. She bit her lower lip, pensively. A strong urge nagged her to ask him to come with her to Ohio, but she realized what an offer like that would do to a man like Cass. If he refused, she knew she'd still have insulted him beyond forgiveness. If he accepted, it would destroy his pride. Either way, they would both lose. No, Laurel sighed. There was to be no last-minute reprieve for her and Cass, no magic words to change their circumstances.

Overcome with tenderness, she reached forward and planted a light kiss on his nose. "Wake up, sleepy head."

Cass opened his eyes. "I'm awake," he said soberly.

"You're a fantastic lover," Laurel confessed, "but it's getting chilly in here." As if to prove her point, she shivered violently.

Rubbing his hands briskly up and down her arms, he agreed.

"You do feel cold. Come on. Let's go to bed." They were halfway to the bedroom before he added the words that drove Laurel's chill to her heart. "I have to get an early start in the morning."

She clasped his hand tightly, letting him lead her into the darkened room. The sheets were cold, but his body warmed them as they lay in each other's arms. "I don't want you to let Rob chase you off," Laurel said.

"It's better this way, love. He won't make a scene if I'm gone, and your friend Joan will understand about Frank, I'm sure." Cass paused, thoughtfully. "How long will you be staying here?"

Laurel snuggled deeper into the crook of his arm. "I don't know." With Cass gone, there'd be nothing for her in Julian. But, neither was there any hurry to return to Ohio. She still had a week of vacation coming. "I guess it depends on the reception I get from Rob," Laurel decided. "I may start for home sooner than I had planned." Finally, her breathing evened and deepened as she surrendered to sleep.

Cass held her tighter. Perhaps she'd be able to forgive him for deceiving her. It had started so innocently, and by the time their relationship had progressed to the point where it mattered, it was too late to set the record straight. He stared at the ceiling. She loved him, but not enough to cast off her old prejudices. When the time came, Cass wondered sadly, would she love him enough to accept the man he really was?

Chapter Nine

"You have my address?" Laurel asked for what must have been the tenth time.

Cass swung the pack to his back. His breath condensed in a cloud from the chilly morning air as he said, "Yes. I won't lose it, I promise."

"You'll keep in touch?"

He nodded.

"Aren't—aren't you going to kiss me good-bye?"

His eyes raked over her shivering form. "I don't dare," he said raggedly. "I'd never be able to go."

"Cass?"

"Laurel, please," he said. "This is the best way, you know it is." He touched her cheek tentatively, sorrowfully. "Good-bye, love."

Laurel's feet were rooted to the porch by some force greater than her desire to run after him. The sun shone through the branches of the trees, illuminating his path with ethereal beams. The scene was surreal, a dream, a cross between a fairy tale and a nightmare. He couldn't really be going. It was like

WINTER'S PROMISE

watching a stranger trudge down the hill toward the crossroads, his big Newfoundland trotting by his side.

Laurel opened her mouth to call after him, but no sound emerged. Hollowness was the closest she could come to defining the ache she was feeling. Life without Cass. Shaking her head, she watched until he was out of sight, then reentered the house. Her arms and legs were wooden, numb like the rest of her. The breakfast Cass had prepared and left, uneaten, turned her stomach when she looked at it.

Laurel would have preferred spending their last moments in his arms, but neither of them was able to shake off the depression they had awakened to. Both had tried to joke and tease, but to no avail. An all-encompassing gloom had hung over them.

"I wish I could cry," Laurel whispered into the emptiness, but no tears came. It was as if all feeling had left with him when he walked away.

Standing in the middle of the living room, she bid good-bye to the special memories the little house had held. Alone, it was just a dwelling, nothing more. Shared with Cass, it had been a paradise.

The morose look on Laurel's face had been enough to keep Sandy and Dave from asking about Cass.

Rob and Joan found her hard at work when they arrived at the store. After checking the books and records for the previous weeks, they invited her into their office.

"Laurel," Rob began brightly, "have a seat." He motioned toward the extra chair. "The others told us what a great job you did here, you and your friend. We'd like to meet him."

"Thanks."

"You'll ask him to stop in?"

"No," Laurel said stubbornly. Rob deserved no explanation of her private life, and she intended to give none.

"Oh. Well, I see the store ran smoothly without Frank." Rob paused, nervously rubbing his hands together.

"Yes." Laurel could have done without the reference to her old adversary. She felt bad enough as it was.

"Laurel, this is hard for me," Rob continued. "I'm sure Joan has told you about my preconceived ideas regarding professional women." He nodded toward his wife.

"Yes."

"I was wrong," he confessed. "You have it all together. I take my hat off to you. I couldn't be more pleased with the way you handled things here."

Joan was watching her husband's struggle, a sly smile on her lips. "He means it, Laurel," she affirmed. "You know you've arrived when Rob commends you like that."

"She's right," he said. "You're a completely professional person, taking command of the situations that life throws at you without resorting to unnecessary feminine frivolities. I'm proud to have had you running my business."

His compliments cut into Laurel like a scalpel. It was the role she had worked all her life to create, yet

WINTER'S PROMISE

it tore at her to hear it put into words. Closing her eyes, she clamped both hands over her mouth.

Joan was at her side instantly, placing a caring hand on her arm. "Honey, what is it?"

Laurel was silent as unbidden tears welled in her eyes.

Catching Rob's attention, Joan gestured toward the door. Exiting quietly, he left the two women alone.

"Okay, it's just the two of us. Now, tell me what's going on," Joan urged. "You know from experience it helps."

Shaking her head from side to side, Laurel dropped her hands to her lap, clasping them until her knuckles whitened.

Joan pulled up another chair. "Laurel, be sensible. You know how it helps to get it off your chest. You're a psychologist."

Her eyes lifted to Joan's. "I'm not anything, anymore. I've blown my future as surely as if I'd jumped off a cliff."

"Oh come on, honey, it can't be that bad."

Laurel grimaced. "Want to bet?"

Slowly, the whole story unfolded as Laurel told her old friend about Cass. "And then he left," she concluded. "Just like that."

"And you let him? Are you going to marry him?"

"How can I?"

"It's easy," Joan chuckled. "You say, yes."

"No. You don't understand. He's gone."

"That's not the problem, as I see it," Joan remarked. "The question is, do you love him?"

"Yes."

"And do you want to marry him?"

"Oh, Joan, we're just too different."

"I didn't ask for a feasibility study. Do you expect to be happy without him?"

Laurel was desolate. "No."

"Has it ever occurred to you to give up your career for love?" Joan asked. "I did, and I've seldom regretted it."

"But you sometimes do?"

Joan settled herself on the edge of Rob's desk. "Honey, there isn't a person alive who doesn't wish for an occasional change. But I use my training every day, in one way or another. Maybe someday, I'll go to work away from the store. For now, I'm happier than I've ever been. A piece of paper with a gold seal and a fancy frame is no substitute for a man who really loves me."

Smiling at her friend's candor, Laurel said, "I never understood you before. Both of us had always been so practical until you teamed up with Rob."

"And we'd been lonely, remember?"

"And lonely," Laurel echoed. For a moment she allowed herself the luxury of envisioning a life with Cass. The picture lacked clarity of purpose, yet it overflowed with happiness. To be married to Cass was what Laurel wanted, more than life itself. He *was* her life. She would make loving him her career. To hell with Ohio, and degrees, and—"Joan!" she gasped, jumping up, "I've let him get away. I have no idea where he went."

"And if you knew?"

"I'd go after him!"

WINTER'S PROMISE

Reaching into the desk drawer, Joan grabbed several key rings, sorted through them, and tossed one to Laurel. "Then go," she urged. "Find him."

Laurel nervously jiggled the keys. "What about Rob? This is the key to his truck, isn't it?"

"You let me worry about him," Joan volunteered. "Get going before your Cass is too far away."

"Thanks," she said, hugging Joan in her elation. Laurel grabbed her purse, ran out the back door to jump into the dusty white pickup, and backed tentatively into the street.

Which way? Borrego? Why not? Laurel thought. The last time she'd been on foot and she had found him. If she missed him on one road, she'd have plenty of time to search the others. They'd be together again—soon. Whatever the future held for her, Laurel knew it included the rugged, bearded man whom she loved with every cell in her body.

Quickly calculating mileage, Laurel drove down the highway toward the blossoming desert until she was well past the distance of one day's travel for a man on foot. It would still be all right. She'd backtrack, take another road, and find him there.

The twisting, turning road that led to the town of Banner clung narrowly to the canyon walls. Laurel was ready to turn back long before she found a place to pull off and retrace her steps.

One more chance. She had tried all the ways out of Julian except the one Cass had entered by.

Darkness had fallen over the gently sloping hills by the time a weary Laurel parked the truck in Santa Ysabel. There was a pay phone under a glaring yellow light. She would call Joan, tell her she was okay, then go back to Julian. Maybe Cass had called there, looking for her.

"Hello." Joan's voice was anxious.

"Hi," Laurel said, "it's me."

"Where are you? Did you find him?"

"I'm in Santa Ysabel, and no," Laurel replied. "I thought maybe he had called you."

Joan paused, "No, honey, he hasn't."

Exhausted, Laurel leaned against the glass-walled booth. "I'm beat," she said. "I think I'll see if I can get a bite to eat in the café here, then start home. Maybe someone has seen him around."

"Good luck."

"Thanks," Laurel said, hanging up. She breathed deeply, her earlier confidence ebbing. If this place was anything like all the others she had visited in her search, no one would be of any help. It was as if the ground had opened up and swallowed Cass. Or, she thought desperately, as if he'd never existed and their love had been a figment of her vivid imagination.

Slowly, unwilling to face another disappointment, she walked toward the café door.

"The man, maybe," the bartender told her, "but I didn't see no dog."

"That the fella that was lookin' for his big black dog?" a grizzled old man at the bar asked.

"That's him!" Laurel exclaimed. "It has to be. A man with a brown beard and a backpack. The dog's a black Newfoundland. Were they here?"

"Well, I don't rightly know," the old man said.

"He come in here and ate, asked us to keep an eye out for his dog, and left."

"The dog wasn't with him?"

"Nope. Said his dog run off. He hung around for a coupla hours, then caught a ride with somebody in one o' them flashy little sports cars. Red, it was, as purty as the little lady drivin' it."

He'd hitchhiked—with a woman. Laurel was crushed. There was no way she'd ever find him now. "I don't suppose any of you have seen the dog," she said flatly.

Half a dozen heads wagged from side to side. Whatever appetite she thought she'd had, was gone.

Following the green and white marker signs, Laurel drove slowly back to Julian. At night, a black dog would be next to impossible to see. To make matters worse, a storm was brewing. Perhaps, in the morning, she could borrow the truck again and search for Bear. How could his master abandon him like that? Cass seemed to be growing rather accomplished at leaving those he professed to care for. Did she really know him at all?

It doesn't matter, her heart reminded her. If you found out he were an escaped criminal or a bigamist or even Jack the Ripper, you'd still love him completely. "He might disappoint you, Laurel," she told herself, "but he'll always be the love of your life." If I find him, she thought desperately, if I ever find him.

Joan and Rob's little house glowed warmly through the drizzling rain, its windows beckoning to her.

"Oh, Laurel," Joan exclaimed as soon as she'd opened the door, "he called!"

Laurel's heart leapt, pounding in her temples. "What did he say?"

"Oh, well, it's not so much what he said as the fact that he called." Joan waited, sorting her words. "The dog ran away," she continued, "and he thought it might have come back here."

It had been Cass in the bar in Santa Ysabel. "That's all he said? No message?"

"He'll call back," Joan assured her. "I know he will. Why don't you stay home tomorrow? After all, this is still your vacation."

"I wasn't sure you'd want me to stay at all," Laurel said, her eyes darting to Rob. "I was going to make a flight reservation for Wednesday."

"Nonsense," Rob spoke up. "We both want you to stay as long as you like." He put his arm around his wife. "Joan has told me the whole story. If there's anything else we can do, just ask."

Laurel shook her head, pretending to warm herself by the fireplace to avoid watching their happiness. If Joan could find contentment with Rob, certainly she and Cass had a chance. Raindrops dripped slowly down the windowpanes, mirroring the salty tears rolling off her cheeks to drop unnoticed on the stones below. "Dear Lord, just give me one more chance to see him," she whispered, with the clear conviction remembered from childhood.

Harsh winds built the rain into a punishing torrent, beating on the roof and driving it in sheets against the windows. Above the noise of the storm, a scratching at the door went unheeded until they heard the deep, resonant bark.

A little squeal escaped from Laurel as Rob opened the door to the soggy, shivering dog.

"I think it's for you," he teased. "A friend of yours?"

"Bear!" she yelled, dropping to her knees to hug the wet Newfoundland.

Joan brought an armload of towels and they all set to work drying their massive guest.

Laurel ruffled the soft, black, drooping ears. "You love all this attention, don't you, old boy?"

Obligingly, Bear rolled on his back, offering his underside for drying.

The phone beside Rob jangled and he answered on the first ring. Extending the receiver to Laurel, he said, "This one's for you, too."

Her hands flew to her throat. "Cass?" she said tentatively into the mouthpiece.

"Laurel? Uh, Bear's missing," he said haltingly, "and I thought maybe . . ."

"He's here, Cass," she reassured him. "He's wet, but otherwise he's fine." She barely heard his next words.

"And you?"

She wanted to scream, "I'm miserable. I love you so much I hurt. I spent the day looking for you," but she didn't. "I'm fine, Cass," she said. "How are you?"

"I'm okay," he lied.

If she could only see him. It was no good telling him her decision over the phone. If he'd changed his mind, she would be able to tell by observing his reactions when she agreed to marry him. She had to see him. Laurel wracked her brain. How? Then it hit her—Bear.

"I think I can borrow Rob's truck to bring Bear back to you, if you like," she said, a glance at her friends confirming the favor. "Yes, he says I can."

"I take it you and Rob worked out your differences."

"Yes. Everything's fine."

"Good. Look, it's too dangerous to try a trip in this storm," he said protectively. "Wait until it clears. Maybe tomorrow."

He was going to tell her where he was! Laurel had the chance she had prayed for.

"Do you know where the observatory is?" he asked.

Laurel covered the receiver, turning to Joan. "The observatory?" she whispered.

Joan nodded, "I can get you a map."

"Yes," Laurel told Cass, "I'll find it."

"Tomorrow morning around eight, if it's not raining," he instructed. "The gate is kept locked until nine during the week, but honk your horn and I'll let you in."

"You'll be there? Inside?"

"Yes," he assured her. "I work here."

A job? So quickly? "How, how wonderful for you," she stammered. "Is it a good job?" The question was asked innocently, but it came out sounding like the old Laurel, the educated snob. She winced.

"Yes, Ms. Phillips," he said stiffly. "You'd be proud of me. It's a very good job."

"I—I didn't mean it the way it sounded," Laurel corrected. "I just wanted to be sure you'd be provided for." The more she said, the worse it got.

WINTER'S PROMISE

"I can take care of myself, Ms. Phillips," he announced. "Just as you can take care of yourself."

But I don't want to anymore, she thought wryly, and now it sounds as if you don't want me, either. Did he? Laurel couldn't bring herself to ask. Not over the phone. Tomorrow would tell. By then, she'd either be in Cass's arms or on her way back to Ohio. Her breath caught in her throat and a strangled sob escaped before she could cover the receiver.

"Laurel! What is it?" His voice finally betrayed his emotional state, "Laurel, answer me."

"I—I'm all right, Cass," she said quietly.

"You're sure?"

"Positive. You know me," she quipped lightly, unable to deal with his serious tone on an equal level.

"Yes, love, I know you," he said softly. "Very well. Remember?"

Remember? How could she forget? His body was branded in her mind for all time, his heart and soul more precious to her than herself. Laurel sank into the chair by the phone. Rob and Joan had discreetly left the room.

"Yes, Cass," she whispered, cradling the receiver. "I remember. I'll always remember."

"I will, too. Promise you'll come to me tomorrow, Laurel. Please?"

"I'll come."

"Okay. Until then," he said.

"Till then," Laurel whispered. She clasped the phone even after she heard the click that signaled a broken connection. Cass wanted her to come. He'd be waiting. They still had a chance.

The dreamy look in Laurel's eyes told Joan most of what she wanted to know. "He's at the observatory?" she asked.

"Yes," Laurel said. "He's working there."

"Doing what?"

She shrugged. "I don't know. I didn't ask. Probably as a caretaker, since he has a key to the gate." Laurel smiled. "Do you suppose there's a place there for a psychologist pushing a lawnmower next to her husband?"

"You're getting married?"

"Well, not exactly," Laurel grinned. "I haven't proposed yet." She grew more serious. "I hope he still wants me."

"You're ready for a simpler, less prestigious lifestyle?" her friend asked.

"You bet. I've had it with titles and degrees and eggheaded colleagues," Laurel said freely. "It will be marvelous to leave all that behind and live with someone like Cass. I'm glad he's nobody special, except to me. That way I won't ever have to share him. I can hardly wait to see him and tell him the news."

A pioneer's lady, she mused. Once she'd said she'd never fit that mold, and now Laurel found herself wanting that life more than any other. Cass would be so surprised when she told him.

Chapter Ten

Laurel awoke to the sun streaming through her window. Glorious! Nothing could stop her now.

She would wear her jeans, for Cass, since the tight denim had had such a marvelous effect on him. A silly smile lit her face, a warm blush following. *Everything* she wore would be just for him, even her wispiest lacy underthings. And a sweater, as clingy and sexy as the jeans. Laurel giggled nervously. Cass was right, she decided, I am a shameless hussy. Oh, but I love him so, she told herself, warming again at the thought.

Breakfast was out of the question. Bear shared her excitement, hardly objecting when she anchored him in the middle of the pickup bed, with a rope through his collar.

"I'm sorry, boy," Laurel said to the eager animal. "I don't want you jumping out and getting hurt."

According to Joan's directions, Laurel saw she'd have a rather arduous drive. The distance wasn't particularly great, providing you could soar with the eagles. The map lying beside her on the seat showed that it was a long series of turns and switchbacks as the road dropped down to Santa Ysabel, then climbed to over five thousand feet at the observatory. Joan had told her to keep a sharp lookout and she'd catch a glimpse of the white, twelve-story dome housing the enormous telescope. What she really wanted to see was her almost-six-foot man. The observatory was secondary. Definitely secondary.

Laurel was early, but nothing on earth could have persuaded her to delay the start of her trip. She took a deep breath and turned the key. The engine responded with a roar not nearly as loud as the thudding of her heart.

Shifting gears and accelerating, she glanced in the rearview mirror. Bear was fine, his ears standing away from his head like wings as he faced the wind whistling over the cab of the truck. So far, so good, she thought.

There were only two major directional changes in her plans, and she successfully negotiated the first at Santa Ysabel. She was supposed to see a large lake, bear to the left, make one more turn, and the road would take her straight to the observatory grounds.

Laurel swallowed hard. "I'll bet I'm not this nervous on my wedding day." Her hands had been gripping the wheel so tightly her fingers ached. One hand at a time, she pried them loose, wiping her sweaty palms on her jeans, and shook her hands to restore circulation.

"Oh, Cass," Laurel whispered into the empty air. "Want me. Please, still want me."

WINTER'S PROMISE

There was the lake, right on cue. She nearly missed her second turn. The corner was sharp, and Bear struggled to keep his balance, thudding against the truck bed. Laurel felt a stab of panic at the thought that he might have been hurt. As soon as she found a safe place, she pulled off the road and parked.

Bear was fine, looking at her as if he expected to be released to bound over the hills, as usual.

"No, boy," Laurel told him, "I don't dare let you go. You're my ticket to see Cass, and I'm not about to lose you." Or him, she added silently. She could see why Cass loved the outdoors. Crisp, clean air filled her lungs as she stretched her weary body and her tenseness began fading. "If we were out for a Sunday drive, Bear, I'll bet I wouldn't be tired at all," she mused, gazing appreciatively at the lovely wild flowers carpeting the hills.

At her feet were pale, violet-colored flowers. Nearby, a patch of deep green and yellow caught Laurel's attention. Dandelions! Perfect, she decided instantly, the most eloquent gift she could possibly take to Cass.

Carefully, she plucked a bouquet of the fragile-stemmed dandelions. If words failed her, she'd hand him the flowers. She knew he would understand.

Climbing back into the driver's seat, she placed the little cluster by her map. Feeling her muscles already beginning to tie back into knots, she massaged her neck while her mind fought a losing battle with her wildly erratic emotions.

"Lord, I'm scared," she whispered. "This has to work out. It just has to."

Several minutes passed before Laurel could bring herself to switch on the engine, put the truck in gear, and proceed up the hill.

A six-foot chain link gate barred her way, and an attached sign announced the hours the observatory was open to the public.

Cass had said to honk, but she hesitated to disturb such a subdued, private-looking community. Cottages within blended gracefully with the tall pines and natural mountain growth. Somewhere in the midst of the wooded grounds was, as Joan had explained to Laurel, the largest telescope in the United States. To think, she might get to stay there with Cass and maybe even sneak a peek at some of the astronomical equipment when no one else was around.

A glance in the rearview mirror showed Laurel that her passenger was still aboard, but getting very excited. Her own face reflected an eagerness coupled with an obvious strain. She smoothed her hair.

The motor idled and Laurel checked her watch. She was almost half an hour early. Raising her hand, she was about to touch the horn when a man stepped out from behind the bushes and approached the gate. His coat collar was turned up, and he had hair like Cass's, but no beard. He did seem familiar, though. All men have begun to remind me of Cass, she mused nervously.

Stooping over the lock, the man opened it and swung the gate in.

Laurel drove through, carefully avoiding the gate-

WINTER'S PROMISE

posts. She rolled down her window and looked up to ask about Cass.

"Hello, Laurel," he said quietly.

"Cass! What . . . ?" His beard was gone. She was speechless and could only stare at him.

"I decided to take your advice," he said, stroking his clean-shaven cheek, "and conform to a more moderate image."

"You've gone establishment," she squeaked.

"Sort of. It's part of what I wanted to tell you, Laurel. Bear provided the perfect chance to ask you to come here, but even without that, I'd intended to invite you. I'm glad you came," he added softly.

Laurel's fingers curled tensely over the edge of the door. "So am I."

The big, gentle hands she remembered so well settled lightly over hers, Cass's eyes burning into her with an unspoken plea.

"Oh, Cass, I—"

He interrupted, echoing her innermost longings. "I know, love. Me too."

Laurel had been determined she wouldn't cry, wouldn't lose her composure, but seeing him, having him touch her again, was almost too sweet to bear. Laurel blinked back the tears.

Cass broke the spell with understanding. "Why don't you park the truck? I'd like to start by showing you around the grounds."

"I'd love to see them," she replied, glad for the diversion. "Are you sure it's all right?"

"I'm sure," he said, gesturing toward a nearby

parking place into which she smoothly guided the pickup.

Cass reached into the back and released his dog. Laurel watched their loving reunion with joy, then he turned back to her.

She was holding the drooping bunch of dandelions. "They don't keep too well," she apologized, "but I think you get the idea."

"You'll take me? As I am?" He gave a loud cry of joy. "No matter what or where?" Cass's eyes spoke volumes more.

"Yes," she whispered. "I can be a psychologist for any number of bosses, but I can only be happy as the wife of one man."

Opening his arms, Cass waited, holding his breath. Laurel had come to him in complete trust, without knowing anything else about him. Total abandon and total love had brought her. She was his.

Laurel threw herself at him, her arms clasping his neck as he swung her around in delirious joy.

"Oh, love, you'll never be sorry. I promise."

"Seems to me you said that once before," she teased, "and you were right."

A long, slow kiss celebrated their love before Cass lowered her to stand beside him. "What did it?" he asked happily.

It would be a pleasure to tell him. He'd be so proud of her new goals. "I've given up on the superficial world of academics," she beamed. "I'll be thrilled if I never see the inside of a college, or another so-called educated person again."

Cass gripped her shoulders. "No, Laurel. I never

WINTER'S PROMISE

meant for you to do that. It was your priorities, that's all. There's nothing wrong with being a psychologist. I'm sure you're a good one, but you had excluded everything else."

She smiled broadly. "Now I'm willing to be nothing except your wife." His puzzling expression troubled her. Perhaps it was simply the absence of his beard that made him look so different. "I do miss your fuzzy kisses, though," she said, tracing the edge of his jaw with her finger.

"Laurel," he groaned, "you don't understand. I told you, I work here."

"I know. That's okay. I can help you."

"What?"

"I'm not helpless. I can push a lawnmower or trim the shrubs or whatever you do."

"Laurel!"

What in the world was the matter with him? She drew back, puzzled and a little frightened.

Rolling his eyes heavenward, Cass paced back and forth in front of her, driving his fist into his palm.

"You'd better lock the gate, Cass," Laurel observed, "another car just drove in."

Wild-eyed, he acknowledged the car as it drew up next to them and a smiling man leaned out, extending his hand in greeting. "We've all missed you, John," the driver said. "Good to have you back. As I always say, this place isn't up to snuff without our famous Dr. Cassidy at the helm."

"Thanks, Charlie. It's good to be back," Cass said, shaking the offered hand.

Stupefied, Laurel watched the exchange, her earlier smile fading completely. Doctor? Cass? *Her* Cass? Impossible. He had told her—What had he told her? Nothing, she realized. He had simply sat back and allowed her imagination to fill in the details of his life. There hadn't been one word of truth in him. Not one honest word from his mouth.

The dandelions fell from her fingers into a sad jumble at her feet. What a fool he had made of her and how eagerly she had helped! If all the rest was a lie, why should she believe he loved her? She should never have come here, chasing him like a, a . . . Well that mistake, of all those she had recently made, was the easiest remedied.

Cass's firm grip stopped her as she tried to climb back into the cab of the truck.

"Let me go."

"I promised you a tour of the grounds," he said firmly. "And a promise is a promise."

"How would you know?" she hissed. "Promises don't seem to mean much to you, *Dr.* Cassidy." Her voice rose angrily. "I don't know you at all, do I?"

"I asked you here so I could explain myself," he said calmly. "Let me."

"You asked me here to bring you your dog."

"You're forgetting something. You're still thinking of me as a derelict. I have a car, Laurel. I could easily have come to Julian for Bear."

Laurel sighed, gathering her courage. "I came here to agree to marry the man I loved," she insisted, "but you're not that man."

"Yes, I am, love. I can show you."

"And you expect me to believe you, just like that?"

She snapped her fingers in the icy air, wresting her arm from his hold.

"Yes, I do."

"Would you like to throw in Santa Claus and the Easter Bunny while you're at it? They've got about as much credibility as you do right now."

"Probably more, but I'd still like to try." Some of the forcefulness had left him. He sighed. "Please?"

Now what? If she left, as her instincts told her to, Laurel might always wonder what he had intended to do or say to convince her. His alibis wouldn't work, but by listening she could free herself of his memory. Clear the air, so to speak.

She was going to stay for her own sake, to prove to herself she didn't love this stranger. She couldn't. Her pride wouldn't permit it.

Cass hadn't touched her again, but his presence was enough to stimulate her overworked senses as her anger began to fade.

"This is what most of the tourists see," he explained, leading the way into a marble-floored gallery. Its walls were lined with astronomical photographs, and in the center lay an enormous circular object with a concave center.

Laurel was visibly impressed, and a light-hearted, almost giddy sensation was beginning to fill her. "They're beautiful," she said, indicating the photos, her natural curiosity bombarding her mind with questions.

Slowly, she toured the large room, reading the scientific data with each picture. "And that?" she asked when they reached the center of the room. Unconsciously, she smiled at him.

"It's a model of the mirror on the two hundred inch reflecting telescope. Come on. I'll show you the real thing."

Laurel stifled a giggle, thinking about what he had said. He'd show her the real thing, indeed. Cass was being so serious, so businesslike, while her imagination ran wild, finding ribald humor in everything.

A clear, enticing picture of him—all of him—popped into her mind. Now *that* was the real thing! Blushing and slightly embarrassed, she pressed her fingertips to her lips. Picturing him in the buff had both excited and further relaxed her. It was awfully hard to nurture her anger when she saw him so vulnerable, stripped of all pretense, all protection.

"What's so funny?" He had stuffed both hands into his jacket pockets and slowed his pace to equal hers.

Laurel shook her head. "Private joke," she chuckled.

"Oh."

Cass seemed so different to her. Perhaps it was this environment; perhaps it was the loss of his beard. No. Something else. Mood? That was probably closer to the truth. His good humor, which had warmed and encouraged her before, was totally absent. No hint of a smile had teased his lips since she'd arrived. It would be good to hear him laugh, to see him enjoying life again, she mused.

Cass gestured upward at the dome looming overhead. "This is our chief claim to fame. Used to be the biggest in the world. It's a hard climb, but worth it."

They puffed up the long flights of marble stairs. He had said it was big, but Laurel's first sight of the giant, two hundred inch telescope took her breath away. She froze on the top step leading to the viewing gallery. Enclosed behind glass panes was the most impressive telescope she had ever seen, rising stories above them inside the dome and descending even farther below.

"Oh, Cass!" she exclaimed, "I can't believe it!"

Inching her way to the railing overlooking the monstrous instrument, she felt suddenly dizzy. Reaching for him, she clutched his arm, discarding her plans to stay angry and aloof. "Do they let you use it?"

Cass stiffened, his arm rock-hard, his muscles knotting at her touch. "It's mostly used for making photographic plates and taking other measurements with special equipment, but an astronomer can sit in that cage up there. It's the prime focus."

"What exactly are you, Cassidy?" she asked pointedly, releasing her hold on him.

"You mean my job?"

"Uh huh. How about a proper introduction?"

"John Cassidy," he said, looking out over the huge telescope, his hands grasping the railing. "Ph.D. in astronomy. Also known as Dr. Cassidy, but prefers plain 'Cass' from close friends. I oversee a lot of the research done here."

"I see," Laurel said slowly. "And you live here on the grounds?"

He nodded. "We have a small permanent staff. The rest of the astronomers visit by invitation and stay only a few days. Telescope time comes very dear." He turned, starting down the stairs. "Come on. There's a lot more."

A lot more. How much more could she take? Laurel wondered seriously. The new Cass was beginning to affect her almost as much as the lovable vagabond she'd spent the last few weeks getting to know. Her wandering lover had been charming, and warm, and enormously attractive. That was the man she had come to adore, but this Cass was more. He was all he had been, plus fascinating, impressive, influential, and much more. Laurel found herself developing a first-class case of hero worship.

Other staff members greeted them amiably as they completed their tour of three more major telescopes.

Cass paused. "May I show you my house?" he asked, remaining carefully noncommittal.

"Sure. Why not?" she shrugged. His house. I should see it, she reasoned plausibly. It's probably totally different, too, formal and cold like the home of a stranger. But he isn't a stranger, she reminded herself. In spite of everything, he's still Cass, a small voice inside her whispered, and he loves you. Did he? she wondered. Did he? Everything had happened so disconcertingly fast since she had arrived at the observatory. Her Cass was gone. He was buried within a complex man Laurel hardly knew, a man who was trying hard to impress her with a side of his character that she had once dearly wished he possessed. Was it really so bad? She had envisioned a simple life that would have been foreign to everything in her past. Perhaps it was time to paint a different, broader picture of the future.

They were at the door of the cottage when Laurel snapped out of her reverie.

Holding the door for her, Cass stood aside. His home spoke eloquently of a warmth and depth of character that Laurel had only encountered once before—with Cass.

She breathed a sigh. "Ooh."

"I like it," he said softly, "but it's still lonely."

Yes, Laurel agreed silently. Anywhere is lonely without love. She could still go back to Ohio and only Cass would know what a fool she had made of herself over him. Running her hands lovingly over the back of the couch, Laurel studied the inviting room. And the man.

He had removed his jacket and was standing only a few feet away. All she had to do was run to him and they could spend an eternity in each other's arms. Her gaze locked with his.

"Marry me, love," he said pleadingly, softly.

"You told me a lot of things that weren't true," she whispered.

"No, Laurel, no," he insisted in a choked voice. "I never lied. I know I should have told you more, but every time I waited for the right moment, something else happened to convince me our relationship couldn't stand any more problems. I thought that if you could love me as a nobody, I'd be sure of your love."

Her love? Why did he feel the need to prove her love? He should have known she'd love him with a Ph.D. "Yes," her conscience screamed, "you might have accepted him only because of the degree. You told him so."

Laurel bit her lip, fighting tears, angry at herself for having been so shallow. She had done exactly that. It had been an intrinsic part of her character before Cass had loved away all the old hurts and prejudices. How could he possibly have fallen in love with her when he knew what a self-seeking person she was?

Now he was trying to be kind. She owed him more. "You don't want me," she said stoically. "You deserve better."

"No, Laurel, please. Don't berate yourself. We were both wrong. We can make it work, I know we can. With the childhood you had, I can understand the walls you built, but that's all over now. Let me back into your life. Don't close yourself off again."

She turned away, woodenly reaching for the latch on the front door. Think. She needed time to think. Everything was happening too fast, not at all the way she had envisioned.

Cass didn't try to stop her. There was nothing more he could say, except, "I love you," as she closed the door behind her.

It hadn't worked. Anger and despair churned within him as he stood alone in the deserted room. Closing his eyes slowly and deliberately, his fists clenched, Cass fought the growing emotional tide that threatened to overwhelm him.

"Men don't cry," he reminded himself sarcastically, swiping boldly at the salty moisture clinging to his lashes. God, it hurt. He drew a shaky breath. Whatever he'd felt for anyone before had been nothing compared to Laurel. No other woman had ever brought him to the heights of love she had, just as no other woman had ever been able to cause such excruciating, heartwrenching pain. They'd been so close to making it work. So close.

Turning, he walked away from the front door.

Laurel stood quietly on the porch, her senses reeling. Cass had offered himself in the purest form, without worldly embellishments, and she had learned to love him completely. Now the rest of him had come into view, and the picture she'd had was enhanced. Love? Yes! Laurel gasped, choking back sobs of joy. She loved him so much she felt like she was drowning in the swirl of her emotions.

Unbelievably, he wanted her. Her, just as she was, knowing all about her past failures and biases. How could she offer him less in return?

Her fingers impatiently brushed away a stray tear. She wanted to go back inside, but not looking like she'd been crying.

Smiling to herself, enjoying her feelings of sweet release, and accepting Cass's love, she pressed her fingertips to her lips and stood poised in rapt ecstasy at his door. As her smile grew to a silly grin, she quietly twisted the brass knob and eased the door open, tiptoeing inside.

Laurel walked softly throughout the cottage, investigating each room until one last door yielded what she sought.

Fully dressed, Cass had stretched out on the bed,

his arm thrown over his eyes, his chest rising and falling in an uneven rhythm.

Her heart nearly stopped. He hadn't known she would return! He must have thought that when she walked out the door she was going for good.

Oh, Cass, her heart cried out, open your eyes! Look at me. I'm here!

No noise of movement betrayed her presence as Laurel crossed the room to him and seated herself on the edge of his bed.

"Beat it, Bear," Cass grumbled, keeping his eyes covered and closed. Didn't that damn dog know when to leave him alone?

Laurel stifled a giggle, crawling onto the mattress and nudging Cass gently, wordlessly.

"I said, get off," he growled menacingly, "and I meant it. Move."

She had intended to simply kiss him, but this was too perfect an opportunity to pass up. Almost overcome by her growing mirth, Laurel leaned over, held her breath, and trailed her moist tongue lovingly over his exposed jaw. She was almost knocked off the bed when Cass roared his disapproval and swung his arm to fend off the show of affection he mistakenly thought had come from his blameless, absent canine.

Melodic laughter spilled out of Laurel as she rolled on the bed, near hysterics.

Cass blinked incredulously, his eyes still harboring a telltale redness. "You're back!"

All Laurel could do was nod, gripping her sides and gasping for breath between spasms of laughter.

"To stay?" Relief and ecstasy surged through him.

Again she nodded, tears of joy rolling down her cheeks.

Straddling her body, Cass pinned her hands to the bed beside her head. "Okay, funny lady," he grinned. "Why didn't you just kiss me? Why the slurp?"

Wide-eyed, Laurel looked up at him. "That was . . . that was . . ."—more giggles—"the only part of you I hadn't tasted before."

"Well, almost." His smile broadened. "Tell you what. Stick around long enough and I'll see to it you get to sample the full menu."

"Promise?"

"Promise."

"I love you, Cass," Laurel whispered breathlessly. "Are there any more secrets I should know, or have I seen all the facets of John Cassidy, Ph.D. and vagabond?"

"You mean besides my twelve kids in Pittsburgh and my thirty-two prior marriages?"

Laurel made a face. "Come on, Cassidy, I'm serious."

"I know you are, love," he said tenderly. "I'm just so glad to see you it's made me a little silly."

"A *little*?" Laurel laughed. "You look downright idiotic with that stupid grin all over your face."

"Can't help it, love. You do that to me."

"Among other things," Laurel said suggestively. "But first, I want to hear about your twelve kids."

"Well," he smiled, "I may have exaggerated just a little."

"No twelve kids?"

"No, and no other women. But I still have two

more roles to play for you, love," he whispered in her ear. "Husband, and father of our children."

"Mmm." Laurel pulled his lips closer to hers. "I think we should investigate those personality traits as soon as possible."

"Well then," he breathed against her cheek, "let's start right now."

"THE MOST USEFUL TOOL ANYONE WHO WRITES CAN BUY"

—John Fischer, *Harper's Magazine*

HOW TO GET HAPPILY PUBLISHED
A Complete and Candid Guide
by Judith Applebaum and Nancy Evans
Revised and Updated Edition

All the ways and resources with which to get the very best deal for your writing and yourself including:

—How to get the words right
—How to submit a manuscript, outline or idea
—How to deal with contracts to get all the money you're entitled to
—How to promote your own work
—How to publish your own work yourself
—And much, much more

"EVERYTHING YOU NEED TO KNOW!"—*Boston Globe*

(0452-254752—$6.95 U.S., $8.75 Canada)

Buy them at your local bookstore or use this convenient coupon for ordering.

NEW AMERICAN LIBRARY
P.O. Box 999, Bergenfield, New Jersey 07621

Please send me the Plume book I have checked above. I am enclosing $_____
(please add $1.50 to this order to cover postage and handling). Send check or money order—no cash or C.O.D.'s. Prices and numbers are subject to change without notice.

Name_____

Address_____

City _____ State _____ Zip Code _____
Allow 4-6 weeks for delivery.
This offer is subject to withdrawal without notice.

RAPTURE ROMANCE

*Provocative and sensual,
passionate and tender—
the magic and mystery of love
in all its many guises*

Coming next month

STERLING DECEPTIONS by JoAnn Robb. Entranced by his seductive charm and beguiling blue eyes, Jan Baxter shared a memorable night of glorious passion with Dave Barrie. And though Jan wasn't convinced, Dave called it love—and swore he'd prove it...

BLUE RIBBON DAWN by Melinda McKenzie. Billie Weston was swept into aristocrat Nicholas du Vremey's caressing arms and a joyous affair that tantalized her with the promise of love. But Nick's stuffy upper-class circle was far removed from Billy's own. Was the flaming passion they shared enough to overcome the gulf between their worlds?

RELUCTANT SURRENDER by Kathryn Kent. Manager Marcy Jamison was headed straight for the top until Drew Bradford—with his seductive smile and Nordic blue eyes—swept all her management guidelines aside. And though he broke all her rules, he filled her with a very unmanageable desire. She wanted Drew—but was there room in her life for someone who persisted in doing things his own way...?

WRANGLER'S LADY by Deborah Benét. Breanna Michaels wasn't prepared for the challenge of Skye Latimer—who'd never met a bronco he couldn't break, or a woman he couldn't master—for she found herself torn between outraged pride... and aroused passion....

TELL US YOUR OPINIONS AND RECEIVE A FREE COPY OF THE RAPTURE NEWSLETTER.

Thank you for filling out our questionnaire. Your response to the following questions will help us to bring you more and better books. In appreciation of your help we will send you a free copy of the Rapture Newsletter.

1. Book Title:_____

   Book #:_____ (5-7)

2. Using the scale below how would you rate this book on the following features? Please write in one rating from 0-10 for each feature in the spaces provided. Ignore bracketed numbers.

   (Poor) 0 1 2 3 4 5 6 7 8 9 10 (Excellent)
                                                   0-10 Rating

   Overall Opinion of Book................ _____ (8)
   Plot/Story............................ _____ (9)
   Setting/Location...................... _____ (10)
   Writing Style......................... _____ (11)
   Dialogue.............................. _____ (12)
   Love Scenes........................... _____ (13)
   Character Development:
   Heroine:.............................. _____ (14)
   Hero:................................. _____ (15)
   Romantic Scene on Front Cover......... _____ (16)
   Back Cover Story Outline.............. _____ (17)
   First Page Excerpts................... _____ (18)

3. What is your: Education: Age:_____ (20-22)

   High School   ( )1   4 Yrs. College ( )3
   2 Yrs. College ( )2   Post Grad   ( )4   (23)

4. Print Name:_____

   Address:_____

   City:_____State:_____Zip:_____

   Phone # (   )_____ (25)

   Thank you for your time and effort. Please send to New American Library, Rapture Romance Research Department, 1633 Broadway, New York, NY 10019.

RAPTURE ROMANCE

*Provocative and sensual, passionate and tender—
the magic and mystery of love
in all its many guises*

New Titles Available Now

(0451)

- **#57 ☐ WINTER'S PROMISE by Kasey Adams.** A chance meeting brought psychologist Laurel Phillips and a handsome vagabond, Cass, together in a night of unforgettable ecstasy. But, despite their shared love, what future was there for a successful career woman and a rootless wanderer? (128095—$1.95)*

- **#58 ☐ BELOVED STRANGER by Joan Wolf.** A winter storm left them in each other's arms, shy Susan Morgan and Ricardo Montoya, baseball's hottest superstar. Even though their worlds were so far apart, Susan found her love had a chance—If she only had the strength to grasp it . . . (128109—$1.95)*

- **#59 ☐ BOUNDLESS LOVE by Laurel Chandler.** *"Andrea, your new boss, Quinn Avery, intends to destroy everything you've been working for."* The warning haunted her, even as his sensuous lips covered her with kisses. Was Quinn just using her to further his career? Andrea had to know the truth—even if it broke her heart . . . (128117—$1.95)*

- **#60 ☐ STARFIRE by Lisa St. John.** Shane McBride was overwhelmed by Dirk Holland's enigmatic magnetism as he invaded her fantasies—and her willing body. But soon Shane found herself caught in the love-web of a man who wanted to keep *all* his possessions to himself . . . (128125—$1.95)*

*Price is $2.25 in Canada
To order, use the convenient coupon on the last page.

GET SIX RAPTURE ROMANCES EVERY MONTH FOR THE PRICE OF FIVE.

Subscribe to Rapture Romance and every month you'll get six new books for the price of five. That's an $11.70 value for just $9.75. We're so sure you'll love them, we'll give you 10 days to look them over at home. Then you can keep all six and pay for only five, or return the books and owe nothing.

To start you off, we'll send you four books absolutely FREE. "Apache Tears," "Love's Gilded Mask," "O'Hara's Woman," and "Love So Fearful." The total value of all four books is $7.80, but they're yours *free* even if you never buy another book.

So order Rapture Romances today. And prepare to meet a different breed of man.

YOUR FIRST 4 BOOKS ARE FREE! JUST PHONE 1-800-228-1888*

(Or mail the coupon below)
*In Nebraska call 1-800-642-8788

Rapture Romance, P.O. Box 996, Greens Farms, CT 06436

Please send me the 4 Rapture Romances described in this ad FREE and without obligation. Unless you hear from me after I receive them, send me 6 NEW Rapture Romances to preview each month. I understand that you will bill me for only 5 of them at $1.95 each (a total of $9.75) with no shipping, handling or other charges. I always get one book FREE every month. There is no minimum number of books I must buy, and I can cancel at any time. The first 4 FREE books are mine to keep even if I never buy another book.

Name	(please print)
Address	City
State Zip	Signature (if under 18, parent or guardian must sign)

ℝℝ RAPTURE ROMANCE

This offer, limited to one per household and not valid to present subscribers, expires June 30, 1984. Prices subject to change. Specific titles subject to availability. Allow a minimum of 4 weeks for delivery.

RR 183

RAPTURE ROMANCE

*Provocative and sensual,
passionate and tender—
the magic and mystery of love
in all its many guises*

(0451)
- #45 ☐ SEPTEMBER SONG by Lisa Moore. (126301—$1.95)*
- #46 ☐ A MOUNTAIN MAN by Megan Ashe. (126319—$1.95)*
- #47 ☐ THE KNAVE OF HEARTS by Estelle Edwards. (126327—$1.95)*
- #48 ☐ BEYOND ALL STARS by Linda McKenzie. (126335—$1.95)*
- #49 ☐ DREAMLOVER by JoAnn Robb. (126343—$1.95)*
- #50 ☐ A LOVE SO FRESH by Marilyn Davids. (126351—$1.95)*
- #51 ☐ LOVER IN THE WINGS by Francine Shore. (127617—$1.95)*
- #52 ☐ SILK AND STEEL by Kathryn Kent. (127625—$1.95)*
- #53 ☐ ELUSIVE PARADISE by Eleanor Frost. (127633—$1.95)*
- #54 ☐ RED SKY AT NIGHT by Ellie Winslow. (127641—$1.95)*
- #55 ☐ BITTERSWEET TEMPTATION by Jillian Roth. (127668—$1.95)*
- #56 ☐ SUN SPARK by Nina Coombs. (127676—$1.95)*

*Price is $2.50 in Canada.

Buy them at your local bookstore or use coupon on last page for ordering.

RAPTURE ROMANCE

Provocative and sensual, passionate and tender— the magic and mystery of love in all its many guises

(0451)

- #33 ☐ APACHE TEARS by Marianne Clark. (125525—$1.95)*
- #34 ☐ AGAINST ALL ODDS by Leslie Morgan. (125533—$1.95)*
- #35 ☐ UNTAMED DESIRE by Kasey Adams. (125541—$1.95)*
- #36 ☐ LOVE'S GILDED MASK by Francine Shore. (125568—$1.95)*
- #37 ☐ O'HARA'S WOMAN by Katherine Ransom. (125576—$1.95)*
- #38 ☐ HEART ON TRIAL by Tricia Graves. (125584—$1.95)*
- #39 ☐ A DISTANT LIGHT by Ellie Winslow. (126041—$1.95)*
- #40 ☐ PASSIONATE ENTERPRISE by Charlotte Wisely. (126068—$1.95)
- #41 ☐ TORRENT OF LOVE by Marianna Essex. (126076—$1.95)
- #42 ☐ LOVE'S JOURNEY HOME by Bree Thomas. (126084—$1.95)
- #43 ☐ AMBER DREAMS by Diana Morgan. (126092—$1.95)
- #44 ☐ WINTER FLAME by Deborah Benét. (126106—$1.95)

*Price is $2.25 in Canada

Buy them at your local bookstore or use coupon on next page for ordering.

ON SALE NOW!

Signet's daring new line of historical romances...

SCARLET RIBBONS

In the decadent world of Shanghai, her innocence and golden beauty aroused men's darkest desires....

DRAGON FLOWER
by Alyssa Welles

Sarina Paige traveled alone to exotic Shanghai not knowing fate was sending her into the storm of rich American Janson Carlyle's lust. But even as his kisses awakened her passion, his demand for her heart without promising his own infuriated her.

Sarina's blonde beauty was a prize many men tried to claim, including the handsome Mandarin, Kwen, who offered her irresistible pleasures on his sumptuous estate and the warmth of his protective love. But Janson offered her the dream of fulfilling her deepest desires, and pursued by these two powerful men, she fought to choose her own destiny....

(0451-128044—$2.95 U.S., $3.50 Canada)

Buy them at your local bookstore or use this convenient coupon for ordering.
NEW AMERICAN LIBRARY
P.O. Box 999, Bergenfield, New Jersey 07621
Please send me the books I have checked above. I am enclosing $_____
(please add $1.00 to this order to cover postage and handling). Send check or money order—no cash or C.O.D.'s. Prices and numbers are subject to change without notice.

Name_____

Address_____

City _____ State _____ Zip Code _____
Allow 4-6 weeks for delivery.
This offer is subject to withdrawal without notice.